JACK

SHIFTER VENGEANCE

BOOK ONE

APPLETON WOLVES TRILOGY

Free Book!

Sign up to my email list and receive your free
copy of the prequel *Shifter Strayed*

Sign up here

The sun was shining today in Appleton for some reason, with its long shimmering rays casting over the long rows of tombstones behind the priest. I couldn't feel the warmth of the sun over me. I felt cold, like my body was inside a refrigerator gathering up as much freezing air as possible.

I couldn't see any color. The leaves of the cemetery looked like they were pale and dying along with the tree they dropped from, despite the trees being healthy and plentiful with leaves and a nice colored bark. All I could see was a gray, monotone world with no excitement, no movement, no energy, and no happiness.

The grass was nothing more than withering blades of greenery that are ready to be whisked away by the most violent winds. Maybe it was because of the sunglasses I wore that matched my black, square-neck, sleeveless dress. Or maybe it was because I didn't want to see any color on purpose. Maybe I wanted the world to be dark to match the color of my life right now.

My ears were numb to any sounds. I couldn't hear any birds chirping or any butterflies fluttering nearby. I knew and sensed that they were there moving their beaks and wings and being happy as usual under the radiating sun that lit up their day. But all I could hear was this buzzing sound that prevented me from hearing anything except for the priest delivering his eulogy.

I stood beside my Aunt Carrie along with a crowd of other people who were dressed in black tuxedos and dresses. Some wore sunglasses like me to hide the anguish in their faces, the tears that welled up in their eyes like I had. I held my aunt's left hand and felt the grip and sweat of it on mine, as if she was sending me an invisible message: *I got you, my precious, beautiful, niece and I'm not letting you go. As strong as this grip is on your hand, this is how strong I'm going to be for you, because I'll always be here for you, protect you, and never leave you.*

My Aunt Carrie and I looked at my mother Cassidy lying beautifully under the sun in her casket, wearing a long-sleeved white dress. The sleeves were puffed, and the dress was cotton, lined, and had a long column of buttons in the front. It was the most remarkable white dress I've seen in my entire seventeen years of existence.

Mom also wore the most beautiful white heels I've ever seen. The heels were decked with crinkled bows on top, along with rounded heels and a slim ankle strap. My mom laid in her coffin with her hands placed over her stomach. Her fingers were intertwined together over a small gap between her hands and stomach, where I would place something at the end of the service.

The funeral home beautician took care to make my mom very lovely for her funeral. Her long, blonde wavy hair was straightened, and her cheeks were rosy red. The pancake makeup applied to her face by the mortuary cosmetologist made my mom look like her appearance from when she was alive. The sun's rays shined on her, giving light and color to her already paling corpse.

After the priest was done speaking, it was my aunt's turn to deliver her eulogy of her sister. I saw her shoulder-length dark brown hair bob up and down as she walked to the podium to speak. The smell of her may rose and jasmine perfume wafted by me as she walked up to where the priest was, and I could smell the trail of bourbon vanilla she created while walking past me.

My aunt greeted the crowd and thanked them for being at my mom's funeral. She said that they held a special place in my mom's life as much as she did in theirs. My aunt talked about her sister and how they grew up in foster homes, which made them pull closer together and become inseparable in their lives. Aunt Carrie praised her sister for her drive to be successful in her life as an attorney and for building a life with a family that she loved more than anything in this world.

After talking about my mom, my aunt turned towards me with teary eyes.

"I look at my niece Ericka over there and I can't help but see the beautiful little girl that Cassidy is going to leave behind. Ericka is going to be a high school senior in the Fall and I'm so proud of her, as I know her mother would be if she was still with us today. But my heart breaks for her because she won't have her mom be there for her to help her face the trials of such a difficult year."

I could feel my eyes well up with tears again. My cheeks were wet from the waterfall that streamed under my eyes. It was the reason why I wore sunglasses to begin with, so people didn't see how red my eyes were from all the crying I did the previous night as well as all the days leading up to my mom's funeral.

When my aunt mentioned my upcoming senior year in high school, I thought about how my mom wasn't going to be there for me. Ever since my father died, she was the one who I relied on the most for support and comfort when I would face pre-school jitters about the upcoming year. But now that I'm coming up on my last year in high school, the year I thought was going to stress the fuck out of me the most, I had nobody to turn to because my mom wouldn't be there anymore.

It wouldn't be the same with my aunt. Aunt Carrie didn't know how to comfort me and console me the same way my mother would do every year before a school year started. I know she would try her best, but it wasn't the same without my mom. I was going to miss her motherly words of encouragement, the hugs she would give me where she would stroke my hair to relax my brain and get rid of the stress, and the gentle kisses she would give me so I wouldn't feel any anxiety at all.

I choked up trying to hold back more tears at the end of this train of thought. A female near me, who was a colleague of my mom named Paige, rubbed my back, and placed her right hand on my right shoulder. Paige was a rather tall woman and was probably the tallest female at the funeral. I looked up and saw her caring green eyes look at me with sympathy as her long blonde hair blew in the gentle breeze of the day.

"Cassidy was a compassionate mother to my niece and loved Ericka with every fiber of her being. There wasn't a thing Cassidy wouldn't do to make Ericka happy and put a smile on her daughter's face every day. I'm going to miss my sister dearly. But I know Cassidy has departed to a better place, where God is watching her and protecting her alongside her husband. I hope that God watches over you and your families and protects you from the evils of this world. May God bless each and every one of you. Thank you for attending my sister's funeral."

My aunt walked up to my mom's coffin, where she planted a long gentle kiss on her sister's forehead. Aunt Carrie walked over to me and we both embraced, the both of us crying many more tears as we held each other tight. The hug symbolized how much we needed each other and how much we couldn't let go of one another. After my mom's death, we were the only family we got. We now both know how much we meant to each other.

At the end of the funeral, I placed a flower in my mother's hand. It was her favorite, dark red carnations. She would explain to me that carnations were her favorite because they were the flowers my dad bought her when the two of them met. I knew the two of them would be reunited together in heaven at last.

My aunt was going to take me to her house where I would live. She was now my legal guardian. But before we went to her house, my aunt and I went to my house first. The ride home was filled with emotions as I slumped in the passenger seat against a window while smelling a lavender-scented freshener in my aunt's Chevy Malibu. The cause of death for my mom haunted my mind, and it was the same cause of death for my dad, too. Heart attack.

My mom and I were making breakfast that fateful morning. We made pancakes with oatmeal. All of a sudden, my mom collapsed to the ground while getting the pancakes from the skillet to a plate. I called an ambulance to come to our house and they came in fourteen minutes. They rushed my mother to the hospital, where doctors and nurses tried everything they could to revive her. It was too late.

My dad Jerry suffered the same fate when I was ten years old. It was a snowy day in November, and we were playing outside in the snow on our front lawn.

We engaged in a wild snowball fight that I won handily. My dad and I started making snow angels afterwards while drizzles of snow fell on his ginger beard and hair. But then I saw he had a hard time breathing. He was trying to get off the ground, but he couldn't. I saw him grasping his chest as his heart was giving up on him.

I rushed into the house to tell my mom, who phoned for an ambulance immediately. She ran outside and tried her best to save my dad from CPR when he fell unconscious. Paramedics arrived fifteen minutes later and took my dad away while my mom and I followed in her car. But it was too late. Nothing could be done to revive my dad. He was dead on arrival.

I remembered that day quite well. It haunts me to this day and the memory of that fateful day is stronger than before now that my parents have joined each other in Heaven. I believe there is a Heaven above and that my father not only inhabits it, he's also one of God's angels watching over me. Even though him and I were making snow angels, my dad died in front of me and became a real one. My guardian angel.

Aunt Carrie and I arrived at my house, which is being put up for sale. It was and always will be a lovely house in my eyes. Even though the house had no stairs like I wanted, it was still large enough to contain four bedrooms and three bathrooms. The kitchen was so spacious it contained the dining room in it.

In front of the house there was a "For Sale" sign with the realty company's number and name on it. But the location of the sign disturbed me. It was pinned on top of the exact location where my dad suffered his heart attack. The placement of the sign brought back the memory of that horrible day into my mind and I immediately took my eyes off the sign before rushing inside.

Both my aunt and I planned to return to the house before it was sold to gather a few remaining items and clothes belonging to my mother and me. Aunt Carrie would take all the boxes containing my mom's stuff and I would pack all my personal things into three boxes in my room.

But the more time I spent in my room trying to pack, the more I was vulnerable to nostalgia. Some of the most notable events in my life came rushing to my mind. When I saw height measurements on the east wall near my closet, I remembered all the times my parents would create a sharpie mark above my head to determine my height. They would cheer me on when they saw that I grew a few inches.

After that I went to my bedroom window and looked out at the playset in the backyard. It was a swing and slide, nothing fancier than that. I remembered all the times my dad would push me on the swing while my mom would hold me in her arms and slide with me. The nostalgia had become too much for me. I felt more tears coming down my cheeks as I gathered a few remaining things from my room.

After I put everything in the appropriate boxes, I hurried out of my room while tears slipped down my cheeks. My aunt was waiting for me outside and I tried to wipe as many tears as possible from my face so she wouldn't see me so sad and emotional. When she saw me, she couldn't help but give me a hug and wipe the tears off my face. It was at that point that I decided to just let the tears come down from my face.

There was no point in bottling up my emotions and holding them prisoner. I wanted to free them.

I t was my first night at my aunt's house. It wasn't as big as my house, but it was just as comfortable. But what creeped me the most about my aunt's house was that it was mostly secluded, like a cabin with a dense forest right near it. It wasn't Aunt Carrie's idea to buy the place, but rather it was her late husband, my Uncle Aaron, who liked it enough to buy it.

Two large trays of pepperoni and sausage pizza sat right in front of us while we watched *Star Wars: The Last Jedi*. My aunt and I hadn't seen it since it came out and we planned on watching *The Rise of Skywalker* soon. The steaming hot smell of the sausage and pepperoni entered my nose as I saw the death of Luke Skywalker, a scene that made me somewhat emotional. I've seen enough tragedy already.

I was blessed to live with my aunt, who was the only immediate family I had in this rough. But what made me love her even more was the fact that she dealt with her own tragedy when my uncle died four years ago. He was a firefighter who perished one night when an apartment complex was set ablaze by an electrical wire. He died trying to rescue a trapped family.

Aunt Carrie was honored at Uncle Aaron's funeral and he was given a hero's burial funded by the town council. Here my aunt was trying to cheer me up and comfort me with my losses when she still couldn't get over her own. This made me reach over to her and hug her with all my might, and she placed her arms around me.

"Thank you, auntie," I said in a low voice. "I'm very blessed to have you in my life. I love you."

"Aww. I love you, too. And I won't stop, either. We're going to get through this Ericka. I promise."

After this sweet moment, she and I continued watching the movie while wolfing down our pizza.

2

F*ive months later.*

My senior year started in the shittiest, toughest way possible. Not only did I have to deal with the tragic death of my mom, but my two best friends Hillary Washington and MacKayla Devereaux left my high school. MacKayla switched from Angelwood High School to River Bend Charter School. She was still in Appleton and I would see her from time to time outside of school. But it's not the same anymore.

I always admired how beautiful MacKayla was after she dyed her hair in a salt and pepper color combo. It was one of those features about her beauty that made the boys in the hallway stop and stare at her when she walked by. Some of them would drop their jaws, drop their books, and others would fantasize about dropping their pants. She was that radiant. But I never wanted my light blonde hair to ever have that effect because it would make me feel dirty.

I would sit with her every lunch period and just vent to her about how much some of my teachers pissed me off. MacKayla had good ears and would listen to every word I said. She was my personal Dr. Phil. There isn't a damn thing I wouldn't tell her that she wouldn't comfort me about or hear me out about. I loved her for that.

Damn, it sucked not having her here anymore.

Hillary moved out of Wisconsin altogether. Her dad Lance landed a lucrative job in Virginia he couldn't pass on if someone held a shotgun to his head. It was one hell of an emotional day for Hillary when she had to say goodbye to us. MacKayla, Hillary, and I did so many things in the final days before Hillary had to move. The prominent activities involved movie nights, sleepovers, roller skating, and bowling, where I would beat both of them all the time and gloat in their face because…I was just good at it.

On the last day Hillary was in Wisconsin, all three of us met at a park. We discussed what's next for the three of us and how we would interact with each other after she departed. We talked about long-distance Zoom chats, but there were no other ideas for how MacKayla and I would talk to Hillary.

Hillary begged MacKayla and I to come visit her in Virginia Beach whenever we had the chance. She wanted to see us there every summer, a time of the year which she planned for the three of us to do so many things. But MacKayla and I couldn't promise her anything. We couldn't just say yes and break our promise later on. It would disappoint the shit out of Hillary.

Hillary burst into tears when we couldn't commit to her request. It was a windy day at the park so while the strands of her short, bright blonde hair were blowing with the wind, her tears were also whooshing from her cheeks to whichever direction the wind was going. It was a sight that made MacKayla and I cry.

I don't think Hillary looked at her father the same way after the family moved to Virginia. It was like he committed a crime when he forced her to separate from us. The day after Hillary's family arrived at their new home in Virginia Beach, Hillary talked with MacKayla and I on the phone and told us she didn't really speak to her dad that much. She added that she didn't want to be in the same room as him and just couldn't look at him or be in the room with him.

Even though Hillary was visibly emotional that day, I was also crying on the inside very hard. My mom died and my friends were leaving due to life circumstances of their own. I didn't want to add to the misery even more by telling them how I felt or shedding my own tears. It would've been too much. I blocked any tears from rolling out by building a mental dam to guard my emotions from escaping. It worked until I was all alone in my bedroom and I ended up crying straight into the cover of my pillow.

I am all alone now. Perhaps the feeling didn't hit me so hard until I walked through the doors of the cafeteria. I saw busybodies and carefree students walking around the place with trays in hand and food in their mouths. I could smell some of the food swirling into my nostrils from a mile away. The meat from a corn-dog, the greasy oil of tatter tots and French fries, the patty of a chicken sandwich, and the BBQ sauce that accompanied the way-too-peppery chicken nuggets. The list went on.

I also heard students unwrap their food from the intricately wrapped tin foil as well as the sound of their TruMoo chocolate milk cartons opening up at the mouth. The smell of the cafeteria food drifted through my nose as I walked up to the lunch line and got my meal. I only wanted a chicken sandwich, a cup of fresh fruit, and a chocolate milk carton.

I went to a table at the far east side of the cafeteria where not too many students sat. The students who sat there were mostly pop culture nerds discussing the next episode of the *Shadow and Bone* series. I knew they wouldn't mind me sitting at the other end of their table, eavesdropping on tidbits of their passionate discussion. They wouldn't even know I was there.

Once I landed my butt in the circle-shaped seat, I gripped my sandwich in my hand and started eating. With each bite I took, I realized that they would be taken alone. No one would be sitting with me. Hillary and MacKayla had friends of their own who I thought I would be friends with. But it didn't happen. They just mostly talked to themselves and didn't mind me at all. It was like after Hillary and MacKayla left, they just hung out within their own inner circles.

"Excuse me. Is it alright if I sit here?"

I heard a mild deep male voice speak to me as I drank my milk. I chugged it as fast as possible, my taste buds observing it as quickly as I wanted them to. I looked up and saw this massive-bodied guy with brown spiky pompadour hair and bright green eyes. I fumbled to say something before I nervously asked him to repeat himself.

"I asked if I could sit with you if you don't mind. I understand if you want to be alone."

"Oh, um. No, not at all. Please," I said while I pointed to the seat directly across from me.

I was surprised by the turn of events. I didn't expect anybody would keep me company today or any day in the future. Yet here was this freakishly big but super cute guy who wanted to sit with me and have lunch. I was a little shy when he sat down and looked at me with the most handsome smile I've seen in my life.

"My name is Derek. Derek Bentley."

He reached his right hand out to me for a hand-shake. It was like the beast reaching out his paws to the beauty for a dance. I felt charmed and I shook his hand. I felt his big hand envelope mine with ease but there was something about his hand that made me feel warm and comfortable, like it was a signal that he was a gentle and caring beast.

"Ericka Jones. Nice to meet you, Derek."

"Might I say you look beautiful today."

"Oh, thanks. I didn't do much today. But thanks for the kind words."

I wasn't lying. I did straighten my long blonde hair but other than that, I didn't make any effort to look as beautiful as Derek saw me through his eyes. I wore my ripped jeans and a t-shirt with the Led Zeppelin brand on it that I thought was a little large for my size. I guess he saw more beauty in me than I did with myself.

"Nonsense. You look radiant today."

"Thanks…Are you flirting with me?"

I immediately saw Derek's dimpled cheeks turn red and sweat was forming on his perfectly lined forehead. He looked down at his lunch and rubbed the back of his neck, at which point I felt a little guilty. Derek had a tray of chicken nuggets, a side of ketchup, a group of tatter tots, and a plate of nachos he bought from a separate vendor.

"I'm sorry, Ericka. I didn't mean for it to come out like that. I'm really nervous and I'm just new here. I moved from Washington state and I'm trying to make new friends here. I'm really sorry if you took it that way. I can go if you want."

It was so adorable to see how he was nervously trying to explain himself and apologize for something so innocent.

"No, it's okay, Derek. I think you're very sweet for your compliment. I should say sorry to you for my bad manners. I just didn't think I looked that beautiful today with the little effort I did this morning."

"Well, I disagree."

"Thanks."

Derek nodded and started to eat his lunch. But I

couldn't munch on mine because I was too busy staring at Derek's eyes. They were the brightest green I've ever seen. They were too bright and beautiful for a human being. They weren't normal in their gorgeousness for a mortal man. Derek must have had some extraordinary genes or taken part in one of the world's most rare gene pools. Whatever it is, his eyes mesmerized me.

He put down a chip he had in one of his long fingers and looked at me with a smile, a smile that made me blush mildly.

"So, Ericka. Please, I'd love to know more about you."

I could tell you all about myself in a two-hour documentary or a 400–500-page autobiography. And I'm not even twenty yet.

"Umm...let's see."

I saw him looking at me with the most curious eyes in the world. It was like he was ready to absorb the information I would impart to him because he was eager to know me. Perhaps I'm too eager.

"I'm originally from New York City. My parents moved here when I was two years old because they felt like the city was too busy to live in. I'm an only child to deceased parents. My dad died of a heart attack when I was ten years old, and my mother just recently died five months ago for the same reason. Oh, and I'm a senior in high school."

Derek's eyes grew wide with surprise. He grabbed my right hand in his, at which point I saw a shift in his eyes. They were the eyes of sympathy, sadness, and care. It was like he wanted to absorb the pain and sadness I felt, and I only met the guy like eight minutes ago. He looked like he wanted to give me a hug, where I visualized feeling his six-pack against my body.

"Ericka, I'm so sorry to hear that. You have my deepest condolences. If you don't mind me asking, who do you live with now after the death of your parents?"

"My aunt."

"Oh okay. I thought you might have been placed with foster parents or taken under some type of legal guardianship with strangers."

I managed a meek chuckle from my mouth before I could respond to him.

"No, nothing like that. But I don't want to talk about it. Tell me about you. What can Derek Bentley tell me about himself?"

Derek smirked and took a bite from one of his chicken nuggets, dipping it in ketchup before popping it in his mouth. He finally spoke after chewing it up and digesting it.

"Like I said, I'm from Washington state. I'm also a senior here. But what's surprising here is the fact that you and I are already alike. My parents are dead too, and it's so weird."

"You have my condolences. But what's so weird about it?"

"They died when I was ten, the same time your dad died. What a coincidence."

Geez, you don't have to tell me twice.

I looked at Derek with curious, fascinated eyes.

What are the odds that he experienced tragedy around the same time as I did? But it wasn't a matter that I wanted to explore in my mind or through conversation with him for the remainder of the lunch period.

"Let's change the topic. I don't want it to be miserable for the rest of lunch period. Tell me something positive. What are your hobbies or activities you like to do?"

"First of all, I agree with you," Derek said as he flashed a big smile on his face, making me see his shiny grill.

"Second, I will gladly tell you about my love for horror and fantasy movies, with a little action, too. Like Jeremy Renner and Jason Bourne in action. I also love to read a lot of comic books and manga."

"Ooh, wow, see? We're already different. I'm more of a romance and comedy girl. I also *love* to read paranormal romance novels, without any horror. I love to read about the female hero falling in love with a werewolf or a vampire, or some creature, I don't know. It's always interesting to me."

I saw Derek twitch a little at the sound of the word 'werewolf' and he rubbed his head a little bit. It was like the word gave him some kind of discomfort. I also saw a look of seriousness and anxiety on his face.

"Is everything alright?" I asked.

"Yeah, it's just a back spasm. It's fine. I'm fine... It's great that you love those genres."

I nodded while maintaining a look of curiosity on my face.

Why would the word 'werewolf' triggers a back spasm and how?

"So, what else do you like to do?" Derek asked.

"I'm a really good bowler."

"No way! So am I!"

"Really? Well in that case, why don't you prove to me how good you really are? I challenge you to a game one day whenever you're free."

"You are so on. I'm free this weekend if you want."

"I shouldn't have anything this weekend, either. We'll discuss the plan later."

"Sounds good."

Derek and I decided to exchange numbers as the bell to end the lunch period rang. We said our good-byes and went in opposite directions to our classes.

3

Math sucked. It completely sucked donkey balls. I was in my bedroom doing calculus homework while Aunt Carrie was in the living doing her own work for her job. She was a medical biller and coder, whatever that meant. She wanted me to follow in her footsteps but obviously I would have to do my research to see what they did exactly.

The multitude of numbers in my textbook and on my worksheet tap danced in my head, with each step and waltz they took increasing the headache I had. I was beginning to feel dizzy. The number of complex steps it took to solve one fucking math problem over-whelmed my brain. Enough was enough.

I closed my textbook and shoved the worksheet into my binder before my calculus homework gave me vertigo. I put all of them in my backpack before I had the sudden craving to get a snack from the fridge. I got out of bed and started walking to the door when my brain felt numb.

I can't believe math exists in the first place. Whoever invented it must be rotting in Hell right now.

I walked clumsily into the hallway and smelled the baked vanilla flavored Febreze Plug-in that Aunt Carrie placed in an outlet near my room. It sorts of helped with calming my nerves down and letting my brain relax. I walked through the living room, where I saw my aunt sitting at a small desk in the corner and really putting her head down to work. It was like she was trying to figure out how to make a cat formation from a Rubik's Snake.

I went into the kitchen and opened the fridge to see all the possibilities in front of me for a snack to sink my teeth into. I found a newly bought variety cheesecake platter with an assortment of different flavors, from New York style to turtle. I surveyed the platter and found one slice missing from the strawberry swirl side. I didn't care.

The sight of the platter made my mouth form a pool of water from my taste buds. I took a plastic plate and grabbed two slices, one from the New York style and one from the double chocolate. I didn't sit down at the kitchen table because I couldn't wait to eat the slices. Each bite I took melted in my mouth. The cream, the chocolate chips, and the frosting all melted over my taste buds as I entered taste nirvana.

I finished the New York style slice in less than a minute before moving on to the double chocolate.

"Save some of that cheesecake for me! I have a guest who's coming over this week!"

I heard Aunt Carrie yell from the living room. I couldn't help but roll my eyes about how she couldn't trust me to handle myself around cheesecake.

"I don't need to remind you about how you finished an entire platter in one day the last time I brought cheesecake into the house!"

"I got it, Aunt Carrie! You don't need to go berserk over it."

I went back to my room after I finished my night-time craving and pulled out my history textbook. I was going to do homework for one of my easiest classes at school. I could do the math homework later. It wasn't due until Friday and today was Tuesday. I had seventy-two hours to prepare myself for math by going to a pharmacy and buying Meclizine for potential vertigo.

Unlike math, history was such an easy subject for me. I finished that homework in under twenty minutes. I had the rest of the night to myself. But then, I heard my laptop turn on by itself. I hurried to it with a strange look on my face and opened it. It usually wouldn't turn on unless there was an important notification that I needed to restart it.

I opened it and typed my password in. I saw a notification in the lower right corner of the screen. It was from Skype. I clicked on it and almost went ballistic when I saw that it was a chat request from both of my best friends. This was just what I needed to end my night on such a great note.

I hurriedly accepted the request and turned the video camera on to my laptop. The last time I spoke to Hillary and MacKayla was over a month ago. They'd been dealing with their own life stuff and were probably too busy to start a chat. But I was beyond ecstatic now for an opportunity to talk with my gals again.

We all screamed when each of our video cameras turned on and saw each other's faces. I screamed so loud that Aunt Carrie ran from the living room to my bedroom, almost busting the door down because she thought something had happened to me.

"What the hell, Ericka? I heard you screaming! What's going on?"

"Nothing, auntie. I'm just on a Skype chat with MacKayla and Hillary. Sorry for screaming and scaring you."

Aunt Carrie sighed a breath of relief.

"You should be sorry for scaring the bejesus out of me. Tell the girls I said hi."

"I will. Love you."

My aunt replied that she loved me back and left, leaving me alone finally so I can talk with Hillary and MacKayla.

"Sorry we scared your aunt, Ericka," Hillary said.

"It's fine! Don't even worry about it. Oh my gosh, you guys! I miss you so much! Hillary, I can't even understand how you can let so much time go by and endure being away from MacKayla and me."

"It sucks ass," Hillary said as she sighed a sigh of worry.

Her mood started to get as gloomy and dim as the light fixture in her room. It barely outlined as MacKayla and I were only able to see the upper part of Hillary's shirt, her throat, her face, and her shoulder-length hair. Her dark brown eyes almost looked like they had no color.

"But at least we can still interact with each other!" I said.

"Enough of this missing each other crap!" MacKayla said bluntly. "Think positively, guys. We can still talk to each other. Ericka, I can't wait to see you some day when we don't have school. And Hillary? You and I can always talk on Skype every night. But I can't make any promises."

Hillary still felt gloomy. MacKayla's assurance still came up short.

"I know," Hillary spoke. "But it's just so depressing here in Virginia. I haven't been making that many friends in my new school and it's just been depressing. At least you guys can see each other because you're still in the same town. You guys can still hang out and see each other physically. I don't have anything here."

The melancholic, pessimistic mood of the chat worsened, to where nobody knew how to flip it on its head and make it positive again. But Hillary started to form a small smile, which MacKayla and I could clearly see on her face. It was like she came up with a way to rectify the situation.

"But MacKayla's right. Let's talk about something

positive. So, I talked to my boyfriend Chad and it was an amazing convo."

Chad and Hillary dated for an entire year. He wasn't the most handsome guy in the world. I certainly didn't think of him that way now after I met Derek. Chad had a fuzzy, blonde crew cut and dark blue eyes. He met Hillary at my school when the two shared a biology class and the both of them were clueless about the subject.

It was love at first sight and they helped each other out, after which they wound up passing the class. I was beginning to think that high school had some magical, invisible Cupid running around slinging arrows into unsuspecting people.

Could that happen to me and Derek like it did with Hillary and Chad?

"Well, don't keep us in suspense. Spill the beans, girl!" I said with tenacity.

"Okay, okay. So, Chad and I talked about him moving to Virginia to be here with me."

"Oh, my goodness," MacKayla uttered. "That would be so amazing if he did that! Then you wouldn't have to be so miserable."

"Well, that's just thing. After an hours-long talk…he decided to move to Virginia to be with me!"

Just when I thought the interaction between my girls and I was going to be dominated by dejection and depression, the mood became happy as we got excited for Hillary's news.

"Aww, Hillary," I said. "That's so wonderful, honey. When is he going to make the move to Virginia?"

"Around Thanksgiving."

"Dang," MacKayla exclaimed. "That's quite some time from now. How are you going to be patient?"

"I don't know. I'll figure something out."

"So, if you had this wonderful news to share with us, why were your sulky as fuck earlier?" MacKayla asked.

"Well, I mean…I'm going to be like that until Chad arrives in Virginia Beach. Once I see him, he'll wrap his arms around me tight, kiss me, and make my sadness disappear into an eternal abyss. So, you're sort of right about the whole patience thing."

MacKayla chuckled a little and shrugged. It was then that Hillary decided to switch the topic.

"Enough about me. What about you two? Are you in the process of shacking up or am I the only one who gets to make you two jealous?"

"Don't look at me," MacKayla replied. "I love my independent life. I don't want to give up my freedom for some man. Ericka? You got anything?"

"Well…"

Don't tell them about it. It's no big deal. You and Derek aren't a thing. It's not the time to mention it.

"There is this guy I met in school the other day –"

MacKayla and Hillary began to whoop for me at the sound of my words, easily intrigued by who they thought was going to be my future fling.

"So, who's this future boyfriend of yours?" Hillary asked.

"He's not my future boyfriend. We just met at lunch yesterday, and he asked if he could keep me company."

MacKayla and Hillary whooped again, which made my cheeks grow rosy.

"Would you guys stop that? I'm not looking for a relationship right now. With everything that's happened recently, I'm not in the mood for that and I don't have time for it."

My best friends nodded with neutral looks on their faces. I wanted to lighten up the mood after bringing up the tragedies in my life.

"His name is Derek Bentley and we sat down at lunch period together and ate lunch. That's all."

"Did you guys exchange phone numbers?" MacKayla asked.

"Yeah?"

"Did he compliment you?" Hillary then asked.

"On my beauty, yes. Several times."

Hillary and MacKayla both made captivated faces at the same time.

"Did you guys plan any future dates?" MacKayla finished the questioning off.

"Well, there is a bowling trip we might do this weekend."

"Yeah, this guy is interested in you."

"No, we're strictly friends. Besides, we're going bowling as a challenge to see who's better. It's only a friendly hangout, nothing more. Don't have any ideas in your head, you two."

Hillary and MacKayla looked at each other as if they were saying "Yeah, right," telepathically to each other.

"Well, I think this Derek dude is seriously into you," Hillary stated. "What guy wouldn't be, hun?"

"Thanks," I said. "I guess."

MacKayla looked at her phone and told us it was getting late. Hillary and I agreed and blew kisses to each other before we assembled into an air group hug. We told each other how much we loved one another and that we couldn't wait to talk like this again, all of this before we said our goodbyes.

The chat ended and I closed my laptop. I was going to sleep with a smile on my face knowing that I got to speak with two of the most amazing girls in the world.

I had chemistry class for second period, and it was over. I didn't consider myself to be a science person, but I found chemistry more interesting and less hard to deal with than fucking calculus. *Ugh.* Speaking of, once second period was over, my next class was calculus. I darted out of my chemistry class and to my locker. Even though I hated the subject, I was always punctual for all my classes.

I arrived at my locker, which was located almost in the middle of the big locker block in the hallway just a

few feet away from my second period class. I felt the
cold hard steel of the locker door in my fingers, which
described my attitude towards freaking math in
general – cold, hard, and solid steel.

Once I grabbed my calculus binder and textbook, I
closed the door to my locker and pushed in the lock,
ready to get the worst part of my day out of the way.

"Ericka!"

I heard a loud, high-pitched female say my name. I
turned to my right and I saw Maisy Freeland, a friend
of MacKayla who I had briefly met before at lunch
period back in the Spring term of junior year. I
remember that day well. MacKayla, Hillary, Maisy, and
I were sitting at a table near the stage area and sloppy
joe was the special of the day. I had only exchanged a
few words with Maisy that day and we weren't really
close. She was one of those friends who went off on her
own after MacKayla switched schools. But I guess that
was about to change.

Maisy hurried towards me, with her long, light
brown thin hair swinging from one side to the other. I
could smell her perfume as she neared me, the
fragrance of which was a combination of freesia,
jasmine, and rose. I knew then that it was a flower
bomb perfume.

"Ericka, hey," Maisy said in excitement. "How have
you been? It's good to see you again. I'm sorry if I
scared you or anything."

"No, not at all. It's good to see you too, Maisy. I

didn't expect you to see me like this in the middle of the hallway."

"I know. It's so sudden. The last time we saw each other was in the cafeteria back in the Spring, but we didn't speak that much. We just let MacKayla, and Hillary dominate the conversation."

She was right. I remembered that day when Hillary and MacKayla were talking about the musical *Hamilton* and their favorite parts about it. Neither Maisy nor I watched the thing, so we just let our friends talk about it while we listened and nodded with stupid grins on our faces.

"Yeah, I remember quite well."

I started walking towards my calculus class while Maisy walked with me by my side, being careful about moving out of the way when a bum rush of students was walking in the opposite direction of us.

"So, I know MacKayla, and Hillary left, obviously," Maisy started. "But I'm really hoping that we become good friends. I don't like you being so lonely, you know? MacKayla is a mutual friend, and I don't see us not being really good friends. I hope you feel the same way?"

"Yeah. I would like that very much. Thanks."

"You're welcome! And we can hang out outside of school all the time when you aren't doing anything or I'm not doing anything."

"Sounds good, Maisy!"

The minutes that followed were filled with

awkward silence. I looked at Maisy to see if she was still there and had not gone off to her class without saying goodbye. She was still there with me, walking by my side. But I noticed that her face was cast in nervousness, like she was wondering if she could talk to me about something. She bit her lips, scratched her head, and her eyes wandered wildly anywhere but in my direction.

"Maisy? Is everything alright?"

She finally looked at me with a mild smile and built enough courage to tell me what was on her mind.

"Yeah, I'm fine. But I don't know how to tell you something without intruding on your personal life."

A fusion of confusion and curiosity built in my mind and my face.

"What are you talking about?"

"I'll just say it. Are you alright? How are you doing in your life after…you know?"

"Know what?"

"You know…what happened to you this year… involving your family."

It was then I knew exactly what she was talking about. Maisy was beating around the bush with the subject, thinking she was trying to spare my feelings. I knew what she was trying to do.

"Oh…you mean the death of my mother."

"I'm really sorry, Ericka. MacKayla told me. We don't have to talk about this at all. I just wanted to offer my condolences and tell you I'm really sorry for what happened. I really do hope you're doing alright."

She placed her right hand on my left shoulder and

rubbed it gently. I bowed my head down and nodded slightly, rubbing my neck at the same time. Maisy saw what I did, and her face grew red with embarrassment.

"You have no idea how sorry I am. Ericka, I'm really sorry. I can go if you want –"

"No, no. It's alright. Don't apologize or anything. I understand you were just being respectful, it's alright. It's nice of you to ask how I'm doing, Maisy. You're sweet. To answer your question, I'm doing fine. There's no need to worry about me."

Maisy nodded and breathed a sigh of relief. She managed a small smile after she heard my reassurance.

"I tell you what. Why don't we hang out at lunch period today? I'll buy us both lunch. We can also do something after school, too! We can go to the arcade, the mall, movies, wherever. What do you say, Ericka?"

Sounds fine and dandy, but...

"I don't know," I said with the meekest of smiles on my face. "All those things sound fun, but I don't know if I'll have the time. I'm struggling with my stupid calculus class and I have homework due Friday. I don't know how I'm going to do it."

A light fixture in the hallway that was dim, all of a sudden brightened up. At the same time, a look of enthusiasm and elation formed on Maisy's face, as if she had an idea and the light fixture that wasn't working properly was her lightbulb.

"Why don't we meet up for school assignments some days after school? We can help each other out! I can help you with calculus and you can help me with history and English! Numbers excite me, but history and English put me to sleep. Are you an expert in any of those?"

Am I an expert? Are you kidding? I would have preferred the world be filled with nothing but history and English, and no numbers whatsoever! Yes, I'm a damn expert! And did you just say numbers 'excite' you?

"Those are my two favorite subjects!" I said, managing a small chuckle. "I have A's in those two classes."

I considered Maisy's idea for a brief second before telling her, "I would like that very much. Thank you."

"Yay!"

Maisy offered to take me to the movies tonight before I arrived at calculus, and then we'd meet up outside of school to work on our calculus, history, and English homework tomorrow.

"The movies would be my treat!" Maisy said. "Besides, you could use a change in atmosphere instead of being cooped up in your house all the time by yourself. What do you say?"

She had a point. Tonight, my aunt was having her guest over that she yelled at me to save the cheesecake for. I agreed to hang out with Maisy tonight and her plans for meeting up tomorrow to work on our assignments. My response left a huge smile on Maisy's face and she clapped her hands in excitement.

"Great! I'll pick you up at seven."

The bell was about to ring, and Maisy noticed that on the clock right above my classroom. She gave me a small, quick hug before bidding me goodbye and telling me she'll see me later.

"Be strong, okay?" She said before dashing through the hallway to get to her class.

I donned a smile on my face. I thought my fortunes were beginning to change. Here I was, thinking I was going to be lonely as fuck now that my two best friends are gone. But in their place came this smoking hot, six-pack ab guy with the most beautiful green eyes I've ever seen, and now Maisy Freeland wanted to be my best friend. Who knew?

I breathed a sigh of stress as I entered the calculus class before the hallway cleared of any students and the bell rang.

Stupid piece of shit class.

A fter school was over, I decided to go to the park and unwind, releasing all the stress from life by immersing myself in the beauty of nature. I took a big, long breath and enjoyed the strong citrusy smell of the trees and blades of grass around me. My nose ignored the smell of dirt and decomposing wood that nature's insects munched on.

I held a bag of crumbled bread in my hands. I took a handful of the bread out of the bag and spread it across the ground. I saw the several pigeons and ducks of the park gather around and fight for each last crumb before devouring them with ease. I dropped more bread onto the floor and saw the melee once again, with fluttering wings, the quacking and cooing of ducks and pigeons filling my eyes and ears.

It looked like a retarded activity for a girl like me to do, but I remember the first time I fed birds in the local park. I was five years old that day when I came here to the park with my parents. My dad had a couple of breadcrumbs in his pockets. He took them out and took my hands in his.

He placed the crumbs in my hands and told me to reach my hand out. I was five years old and was confused as hell why my dad would make me do this, and what his intentions were. Then he told me to spread the bread on the concrete ground in front of me and I followed his instructions.

Two Canadian geese frightened the shit out of me a minute later when they came flying in front of me and fought for the bread I threw. I almost suffered a heart attack as I ran into my daddy's arms and he held me tight. I remembered crying so much on his shoulders as he held me and told me it was alright.

"I got you, baby," he whispered in my ears. "Daddy's right here."

I got you, baby. Daddy's right here.

Those words echoed through my heart and mind. I knew my dad was protecting me and was with me in spirit. I tossed the last of the bread and I looked up at the sky. I knew he was watching me carry on with this activity.

"I love you, daddy. You too, mom."

I was looking for something, anything, to help me take my mind off my parents. Right on cue, my phone and the notification sound of a text message interrupted the music I listened to. I opened the messaging app and saw a new message from Derek. I paused the music and saw the message he sent me.

Derek: Hey, Ericka. Just wanted to let you know I'm super stoked for this weekend. Can't wait to see you. Hope you're doing well?

A smile formed on my face, immediately thinking how sweet Derek was for thinking about me and caring for my well-being. I shot him a reply back.

Ericka: I look forward to it! Can't wait to see you, too. We're going to have so much fun. And I will have so much to boast about after our game when I beat the breaks off of you hahaha.

I typed a heartbreak emoji alongside a winking emoji with its tongue out next to my message. I saw that Derek immediately read my message and three moving dots appeared under my message. I laughed and shook my head when I saw his new message.

Derek: You're very funny. Ever thought about stand-up comedy as a career? Anyways, I'll bring tissues for after the game. You'll need them.

I was about to respond when the same three dots reappeared, as Derek was typing up another message. I read the latest message from him and the smile from my face faded away.

Derek: On a serious note, wanna go to a movie after bowling? My treat.

Ericka: Hmm…sounds like a date. Sorry, Derek. I don't want to go on a date yet. I'm just not ready for a relationship yet, certainly not at this point in my life.

After a few minutes where it looked like Derek was thinking of a response to text, and three separate appearances of three moving text dots, Derek sent one message containing two sad emojis and three crying emojis. He followed on this message up with another.

Derek: I'm soooo sorry for asking you that. I always keep saying some dumb shit before I even think about it. I'm really sorry Ericka. Hope you forgive me?

I felt terrible for what I said. I wasn't ready for a relationship with anybody. I was confident and right about that. But I didn't want the shield that I put around myself to block my friendship with Derek. I didn't want that. I wrote a message back to Derek to rectify the situation.

Ericka: No, please. Don't apologize. I shouldn't have been that defensive. I don't want to lose your friendship. You look like you're a very good guy. I would love to hang out with you whenever possible, including this weekend. I'm the one who should be sorry. Everything good between us?

Derek instantly read my message as a worried look developed on my face. I hoped everything was back to normal between us after such an awkward conversation. Three texting dots disappeared and in their place was a new message from Derek.

Derek: Absolutely! We're good. Thank you for forgiving me and understanding.

After I saw the conclusion of Derek's message, which included a smiling emoji, I shot back a response.

Ericka: No problem. Besides, I wouldn't miss the chance to wipe the floor with you at bowling. C'mon.

I laughed at my own quip as I saw Derek writing a message. Once it appeared, I laughed even more and shook my head.

Derek: My gosh, you are sooo funny. Looks like we have Amy Schumer and Gabriel Iglesias in the making over here. On a more serious note, though, I can't wait to see you Saturday.

Ericka: Same here. Ttyl.

Derek: TTYL.

4

The time almost read ten on my phone as Maisy dropped me off at my aunt's house. We had fun at the movies before Maisy and I went to McDonald's afterwards. We both had Double Quarter Pounders with cheese, French fries, and McFlurries with M&Ms in them. I felt like a boulder was nestled in my stomach over how full I was.

I thanked Maisy for the wonderful time we had together, and she drove away as I walked up the pavement to my house. But I sensed something was wrong when I saw that the front door was open. Maybe there was nothing wrong and that the guest my aunt had was just about to leave. But I didn't see anybody, and the door was open for no apparent reason.

My senses were heightened, and a strong urge of vigilance overcame me. My heartbeat faster as I walked up to the front steps of the house, feeling in my instincts that something wasn't right or normal.

Was there an intruder in the house?

I walked to the door and opened it silently, not wanting to alert the possible intruder in the house. I observed that the house was quiet as I couldn't hear my aunt and her guest talking. Silence pervaded the house to the point where my nerves got shaken when I heard the slightest of sounds.

I took off my wedge sneakers to stay quiet and placed them next to the door. I walked to the living room with stealth, peeking behind a corner to see if anybody was there. Nobody was there but I made a few observations. Two empty cups of coffee sat on top of the table in front of the couch. They each had stale coffee stains inside, which led me to infer that the cups were drunk hours ago.

Then I noticed the plate of cheesecake in between the two coffee mugs. I studied it and saw only two slices left on the platter – a turtle slice and a strawberry swirl slice. I took the strawberry swirl in my hand and felt its mushy cream and soft crust. This cheesecake was left out in the open for a while.

I don't know why, but a bad rush of energy overcame me. Something was wrong. The front door was left open, my aunt and her guest were nowhere to be seen, and wherever they disappeared off to, they must have done it a while ago because everything on the coffee table sat there for a long time. On top of that, my instincts told me someone broke into the house.

I decided to go to the kitchen at this point to see if anybody was there, being very careful with my movement. But before I entered the kitchen, I was greeted by a small trail of blood in the doorway. Or at least I thought it was blood. The color of the liquid was dark red, and it was easily noticeable on the white tile floors of the hallway.

The sight horrified me. Someone got hurt here or possibly killed. I wanted to scream but I couldn't allow myself to do that. Whoever broke into the house might still be here and I didn't want to alert them. If my senses were heightened before, they were more so now. Tears streamed down my face as I took small quiet steps into the kitchen.

What if it was my aunt's blood? What if she got seriously hurt?

I reached the doorway of the kitchen, not looking immediately at what's in the room, but rather what the trail of blood leads to. I followed the trail, walking slowly into the kitchen. My panic began to grow as the trail of blood grew. More splotches of blood appeared before my eyes and the more I followed the trail, the bigger the splotches got.

The trail of blood ended right around a corner and I turned that corner to discover the source of the blood. It was the most shocking, horrifying, and grotesque sight I've ever seen in my life. I've only seen murder scenes in movies, but I was looking at a real life, gory scene in front of me.

The body of the guest my aunt had over laid up against a counter with blood splattered all over the walls and on the corpse itself. Blood was splashed against the clothes of my aunt's guest, her face, and her wavy black hair. But perhaps the most gruesome, disgusting discovery I saw was that the guest's heart was missing. All that was there was a chest cavity.

I wanted to scream. I wanted so hard to scream. I only hyperventilated and cried so much as a silent alternative so the intruder doesn't hear me. But even my hyperventilation was too loud for me to keep quiet. I couldn't look at the corpse of the guest. It looked like she was mauled by a wild animal and the sight was too horrifying and gross to look at. I wanted to release all the anguish I was feeling. But I couldn't. I heard something in the house.

I heard noises coming from one of the bedrooms in the house, confirming in my mind that the murderer was in the house. I knew I was smart not to make any noise because I just saved my own life. I wiped a few tears away from my face and went to the counter to grab a kitchen knife from the hardwood block that stored the other knives. I gripped it tight in my hand, feeling the triple-riveted, high-impact plastic in my hand.

I maintained my stealth and kept quiet as I walked out of the kitchen and through the living room to the hallway where the bedrooms were. I heard more noises while I walked through the hallway, which sounded like feet shuffling and someone, the killer, moving an item from one place to the other.

I deduced that the noises were coming from my aunt's bedroom, a thought that drove chills, fears, and everything in between throughout my body. I quaked as I walked towards Aunt Carrie's bedroom, thinking she was in danger. With slow, stealthy steps and extra care, I arrived at the door of her bedroom, my knife raised over my head to prepare myself for the confrontation with the murderer of my aunt's guest.

I counted down from three and kicked open the door, but I wasn't ready for what I saw. My aunt's dead body was in the west corner of her room on the left side of her bed, mutilated and bloody just like the corpse I saw in the kitchen. Her heart was missing. But unlike the guest's body, I knew where my aunt's heart was – in the palms of the killer kneeling right in front of her.

The killer dropped my aunt's heart on to the carpeted floor when I burst in through the door. I looked at my aunt's heart and saw it was chewed up and bitten out of, like the killer was eating it. I then knew where the heart of the murdered guest was – in the killer's stomach. My heartbeat was much faster than normal as the killer got off the ground and stood up, his back turned towards me.

Except it wasn't a male. It was a female. The killer turned around and my face became pale. I felt like the skin of my entire body lost all of its color as I stood in front of the killer, shaking, and frightened by who stood in front me. It was my aunt. My aunt was dead in the corner of her room, and yet she was also standing in front of me, her mouth, and hands bloody. The killer looked exactly identical to my aunt – shoulder-length dark brown hair, two green-hazel eyes, and the exact same body and legs.

It couldn't have been my aunt. This must've been some evil doppelganger. It was then that the killer smiled at me, revealing a large set of prickly, razor sharp red teeth, painted with the blood of my aunt's heart. Afterwards, the killer began to shift in all aspects of its appearance, from the hair, face and skin to the body and legs. The killer shifted in front of me into an entirely new person – me.

Now the killer had long blonde hair with light brown eyes and the same exact body type I had. The killer was now my doppelganger. It flashed its teeth at me again and I saw its blood-stained prickly teeth. I wasn't looking at a human killer. This entity was a supernatural creature from which I didn't know the source of its existence.

The creature held both of its hands up in the air and ejected long, sharp claws out of its fingers. I couldn't help it anymore. All of the emotions and distress I was storing within me were now ready to be let out. I screamed the loudest scream of my life, which prompted the monster to charge at me with its claws. I dropped my knife on the floor and ran out of the house as fast as I could to the backyard, where the forest behind the house awaited me. The creature was behind me in close pursuit.

I felt it catching up to me and I felt its grip on my right arm. It swung me around so it could face me, and once the monster caught up to me, it scratched me on my arm before I repeatedly punched and kicked my way out of its grip. I ran into the depths of the forest in front of after I escaped the monster. I looked at my injured arm and saw the severity of the wound. The blood was trickling down my arm so much that I thought the creature severed a serious vein.

I didn't have a moment to catch my breath as I looked all around for the monster that killed my aunt. It was nowhere in sight. The creature who I thought was in close pursuit of me and was literally inches away from me was now gone. I didn't know where it went. But I soon realized the answer of where it was after I felt a huge weight drop on my body.

I felt something tackle me to the ground and it flipped me around on my back so it could face me. The doppelganger monster wrestled with me for full control of my body. It grabbed both of my arms and I laid on the ground helpless as the doppelganger scratched my stomach, causing me to belch out a large scream that radiated throughout the forest.

I could feel something running down my stomach. It was the blood oozing out from the scratches in my belly. The creature looked at its work and taunted me with a smile, showing me its large prickly sharp teeth. I was ready to meet my fate as the monster raised its claws above its head and was ready to sink them into my heart, leaving me with a chest cavity like it did with my aunt. But then, a loud sound happened nearby.

The howling of an animal bellowed from the forest, alerting the monster on top of me. I could see concern on its face as the howling continued. I listened to the howling more carefully and knew the howling was coming from a wolf. I then looked at the monster, which froze in place and developed a look of fear on its face when it saw something coming.

I tilted my head downward into the ground to look upside down at what was behind me. I saw a big black splotch. It looked like a splotch to me because my vision was blurred when I used the ground to tilt my head up and see what made the shifter look so frightened. At last, the monster got off me and prepared to confront what it looked at.

I, too, got off the ground, albeit slowly and in agony while holding my stomach. I was able to see more clearly now what got the monster so scared: a large, black wolf growling, showing its bare teeth and enormous fangs as it walked towards me and the doppelganger. After it locked eyes with the wolf, the monster showed its teeth to the beast to see which one could intimidate the other.

I studied the wolf with my own eyes and saw that this was no normal wolf. I observed its thick, shiny black coat in the light of the moon and then I saw something extraordinary. It had bright green eyes. I also discovered that the wolf looked like it was about two or three times the size of a normal wolf. I had an instinct that this was not a normal wolf. It wouldn't be confronting a supernatural monster if it was a normal animal.

I watched the confrontation between the two creatures. They both stared at each other with hate and anger towards their eyes. It was as if their kind had a long historical rivalry between each other, fighting for dominance in a human world. But the looks they gave each other didn't last and they both charged at each other.

The wolf ran towards the doppelganger creature at record-breaking speed. It pounced on the shifting monster while the latter tried to swipe its claws at the wolf. But it was the wolf who gained the advantage by jumping on the monster and biting it in its neck. The monster let out a large inhumane scream that roared through the trees and greenery of the forest.

The doppelganger kept scratching the belly of the wolf to release the grip of the wolf on it, all while the beast kept sinking its teeth into the monster's neck. The wolf eventually released its fangs from the monster, and it took the opportunity to flee from the scene. The wolf, despite being weakened, pursued the shifting monster with ferocious speed like it wasn't content with letting the creature go.

I was entirely alone in the forest as I hobbled to a tree and leaned against it while both entities were in the dense forest fighting with each other some more. I was left to reflect on what just happened tonight and where my life goes after the death of my aunt. I pushed my hand into my stomach to prevent any more blood loss.

It was then that I came up with an idea to take off my long-sleeve striped shirt and wrap it around my stomach tight to prevent any blood from flowing out. I sat by the tree, traumatized, and shaking in my bra from what I experienced tonight. My mind was overrun with so many thoughts.

Where was I going to live? What will my life and future now look like? Creatures like the one I just saw exist in this already-cruel world?

"Ericka!"

I didn't think about anything anymore as I heard a familiar male voice shout my name from a distance. I turned my head in the direction of the voice and I was surprised to see who it was. Even though I was crying so many tears that blurred my vision, the light of the moon helped me see the male who screamed my name.

I saw Derek standing over me, wearing nothing but some torn up shorts. I could see his refined six-pack abs and I smelled a scent coming from him that I could best describe as a combination of fur with natural forest dirt.

"Oh my gosh, you're hurt! I'm going to help you, okay? Stay with me, Ericka! Please!"

I did as Derek told me and I followed his voice as he spoke to me to maintain my consciousness. The blood loss was getting to me. But even then, I was able to make one startling discovery. I looked at Derek as he was examining my wound. I was able to look into his eyes and I saw the same bright green eyes that I saw in the wolf.

"Derek...where did you come from? Why don't you

have any clothes on?" I asked him in the weakest, lowest voice I could muster.

"Don't worry about that right now! You're hurt. We need to get you to a hospital or something. Just fucking stay with me! Don't die on me!"

I looked down at my stomach and saw just how bad the scratch marks from the doppelganger were. I also saw gashes on my right forearm and stomach. It was the last thing I saw as I started to fade away. But then, I started to feel like I was being carried. I opened my eyes slightly and I found myself in Derek's arms, carrying me with ease. I was like a feather to him as he carried me in a direction away from my aunt's house.

I could feel the remarkable strength Derek had to carry me in his arms. It was like he possessed super-human abilities I didn't know about. My eyes started to shut down, but I couldn't help but connect some dots together. It led to one question on my mind: if shifting monsters exist and the wolf fought with that shifting monster, Derek just popped out of nowhere all naked, and his eyes matched those of the wolf, was Derek the wolf that saved me?

5

I t was January of the new year and I began it in the office of my therapist. I laid on the couch staring at the blank white ceiling, like staring at an empty void that is my life. The aftermath of my aunt's vicious death was wild; it took a toll on my life and how I lived it. I missed the rest of the Fall term of my senior year because of that fateful night, which traumatized me to this day. I don't think I'll even finish the entire year.

Several flash images of that night replayed in my head. The discovery of my aunt's guest's corpse, and the doppelganger monster feeding on my aunt Carrie's heart in front of her dead body while she lay in the corner lifeless, haunted my mind every second of every minute. I still don't know what that creature was. The only name I could think of for it was "shifter" because it had the ability to shift and change its body.

To add to the mental and psychological damage I experienced that night, I'm reminded of that day every time I look at my stomach. The scars engraved into my skin from the scratch marks of the shifter's claws remind me all the time of what happened that fateful night. Even though the wounds healed up, the marks scratched into my flesh by that soul-sucking monster remained and fed the trauma I was already enduring.

I also thought about Derek. He carried me in his arms to an undisclosed location in the forest after initially thinking he was taking me to get patched up in Aunt Carrie's house. It wasn't until the day after the tragic night that Derek told me he brought me to a cabin he inherited from his parents after their death. He told me he had paramedics come to his cabin to examine me and patch me up, which didn't make any sense because his cabin was in the middle of fucking nowhere. Nonetheless, I stayed at his cabin for a few nights while I recovered from my wounds.

Every night that I stayed with Derek at his cabin, which was about four or five total, I kept thinking about the wolf that saved me from the shifter.

Was it Derek?

This question burned in my mind all the time I thought about him. It made all the sense in the world, a world that apparently contained monsters, after connecting and reconnecting the dots. The eyes of the wolf matching Derek's; the sudden appearance of Derek in the forest, naked except for some torn-up shorts that hid his junk; and the superhuman strength he had when he carried me with ease. I wasn't exactly a light person.

Nonetheless, I wound up staying with MacKayla's family after leaving Derek's cabin. I remembered very well how Derek took care of me and nursed me back to health.

I laid in bed in one of the bedrooms in Derek's cabin. It was a small bedroom that looked eight by nine in size and had a small closet. The dark green color of the walls sometimes uplifted me from my mood. I was glad the room wasn't a black hole or painted blue. The bed was next to the lone window in the bedroom, and I stared out of it all the time to see the sea of trees moving through the breeze under a sunny day.

I just woke up from a much-needed nap and stretched every muscle of my body. I sat up in bed and leaned on my pillow while I stretched my arms out. I didn't feel like getting out of bed and opted to stay and look outside at the forest. I turned my attention to the bandage on my stomach and remembered I needed to get out of bed to change it. But then I heard a knock on the door from Derek.

"Come in."

Derek opened the door and gave me a warm smile on his face. He carried a tray of food, which I saw was a sandwich, a bowl with something I couldn't see, and a third plate that had a salad.

"Hello, how are you?"

"Hey. I'm good. What's that?"

Derek placed the tray in front of me as I moved my legs out of the way. I saw that the sandwich was roast beef with a thick, gooey cheese stuffed in it. I picked up the salad plate and smelled the Caesar dressing tossed in it while the other plate had a bowl of creamy white soup.

"I know you didn't eat breakfast so I thought you might need a big lunch. I ordered these from a local eatery, so I hope you like it."

"Thanks, Derek. You're very sweet and thoughtful."

"Don't mention it. Oh, one more thing. I almost forgot."

Derek hurried out of the room and came back a minute later with a white bandage, a cup of water, and a pill. He placed these things on the wooden table next to my bed and took the pill with the water in his hands. He reached his hands out to me for me to take them.

"Take these before you eat."

"Thanks."

I took the pill and the water from his hand before chugging them down in a matter of seconds. Derek smiled at me before getting the bandage.

"Let's change that bandage right out, shall we?"

"Alright."

I pulled my top up before Derek removed the bandage slowly from my stomach. He and I looked at the scratch wounds and saw that they were still there, big in size, but they were starting to heal and close. But seeing the claw marks retriggered that horrible, horrible night. I took my eyes off the wounds and closed my eyes to clear my mind of that night.

I felt the new bandage being glued to my skin before Derek removed his fingers from my stomach. I heard him sigh a little and looked up at him to see him with a concerned look on his face.

"It's going to take time for those wounds to heal. Time is the key to progress."

I nodded and Derek rubbed my shoulder before he started walking to the door. Derek paused in the doorway and looked at me with painful squinted eyes.

"I know how it feels to lose someone violently the way you lost your aunt. I've lost people who were so close to me in such a tragic, brutal way."

I gave Derek a look of confusion. I was expecting him to tell me what he meant in response to my facial expression, but he didn't. He transformed the agonizing look on his face into a normal look and donned a smile.

"If you need me, I'll be in the living room. Just yell my name and I'll come to you."

Derek walked away and left me to wonder what he was talking about. I slowly picked up the spoon and dipped it in the soup before slurping it in my mouth.

MacKayla's parents ended up becoming my legal guardians after going through a legal process involving filing a petition with the help of an attorney, getting a hearing at the county courthouse, and the judge granting my best friend's parents' legal guardianship.

The Devereauxs welcomed me into their home, and it was the best feeling I could ever experience in the world to basically live with my best friend, who I considered a sister. Now, her family became mine and I managed to be somewhat happy when I found out MacKayla and I would live under the same roof. This was despite the fact that I was miserable and depressed as fuck over what happened.

I expressed my gratitude to the Devereauxs for providing me with a new home and becoming my guardians, promising them to get a job soon to help them with their finances once I got my life under control and learned to cope with the two tragic deaths that I've already experienced this year. They told me not to worry about it and to give me time, since a girl at my age experienced so much loss already. I thanked them for their understanding.

The wait for my doctor was getting to be annoying. *What's taking so damn long?*

I was looking at the white ceiling so much that my vision started to get blurred. It was like I only saw the color white and everything else was a weird, disoriented haze. My therapist, Dr. Rick Limerick, finally walked through the doors of his office. He was a short, stout man with peach fuzz on top of his head while the majority of his hair was to the sides and the back. He also had a small, bloated stomach that stretched out when he walked with his back bent.

"Hello, Ericka. How are you doing today?"

That was a complicated question to answer in a word or two. Hell, I couldn't even answer that in a sentence. I didn't answer Dr. Limerick's question because the answer I would've told him would have been too long and I didn't feel like speaking much. I looked at my therapist and saw his worried face when he observed my silence.

"It's common for a person who experienced so much sorrow and loss like you to not have the energy to speak. I understand how you're feeling. You're grieving the death of your aunt so soon after the death of your mother. You're shocked and traumatized over what happened and what you saw. It's alright if you don't have anything to say. I'm here to help."

Dr. Limerick asked me if I had taken the medication he prescribed to me by my doctor, to which I responded by taking out the empty capsule that used to contain sixty pills of a hundred-milligram Zoloft. I shook the capsule in front of Dr. Limerick to show him I took them all and they still didn't work. I was beyond that kind of help.

"Would you like me to prescribe you more?"

I was beyond that kind of help.

I shook my head and managed enough energy to part my lips.

"The meds aren't working."

"Well, what would you like to happen so you can feel better?"

Many thoughts and answers came to mind about

the doctor's question. For one, I would like to go back in time to that fateful night so I can refuse Maisy's offer to hang out. I could've stayed at home and just stayed in my bedroom so that if and when my aunt needed me, I would've been there for her. I could've prevented Aunt Carrie's and her guest's gruesome deaths just by my mere presence in the house. The shifter would have avoided coming into the house if it saw too many people there, especially me as a witness to its crimes.

Then I thought about going back in time to prevent my birth into such a miserable life or preventing my mom and dad from suffering their fatal heart attacks. But then, one final thought crossed my word. In fact, it was one word: Revenge. What if I got revenge for my aunt by finding and massacring the shifter who killed her? Maybe that would make me feel better.

I answered Dr. Limerick's question with a shrug and shook my head again. Even he was getting depressed just by looking at me. He must've thought there was no help for me, except he didn't know vengeance was on my mind. Maybe that was the solution.

"I want you to take solace in the fact that you're surrounded by people who love you and care about you, Ericka. The current living situation with your new family is perfect because they'll give you all the support and love you need to heal. Your legal guardians will ensure that with time, you'll absolutely heal from the travesties you've experienced in your life."

I nodded as my response to what he said. He was right about that. Even though I was very emotional and depressed when the legal guardian process took place, I was happy for a brief period of time when I found out I was going to live with my best friend. That is until all the trauma and all the haunting flash images of that fateful night came back to me.

"You also have me, Ericka. I'm saying this not just as your therapist, but as a friend. You have my phone number if you need to contact me or if you need someone to talk to. I'm here for you."

"Thanks," I said in a low voice after I gave my doctor a nod of understanding.

I sat on a park bench alone later that day and just consumed the natural atmosphere of the park. I didn't listen to any music or feed any birds. I didn't want or have the energy to. I just felt like gluing myself to the bench and sitting there for an unlimited time, reflecting on the direction I needed to take my life into.

My phone vibrated and I took it out of my pocket to see what it was. I received a text message from Derek telling me he was here in the park. I got up from the bench and looked for him. I saw him strolling to the bench, after which I waved at him. Once Derek came to my bench, I greeted him, and he embraced me in his arms.

We felt each other's warmth as I wrapped my arms around his shoulders, and he hugged me tightly around my back. The warmth I felt from Derek was not something I felt for a long time. The last person who gave me this type of comfort was my dad. I didn't have this type of comfort from MacKayla or Hillary. Maybe it was because of their size; the two of them were small like me. Derek had a large stature…kind of like a wolf.

"Thanks for seeing me," I told Derek as we sat down.

"Are you kidding? Of course I would see you. I'm here for you. Anytime and anywhere. You know that."

"Thanks," I said, forming a smirk on my face. "I appreciate your support."

"So, what did you want to see me about?"

"I've had a lot of time for myself to think about what to do next in my life. Both of my parents died of heart attacks, as you know already. I can't bring them back to me or avenge their deaths. But my aunt died a gory, horrible death and I can't bring her back, either. But I can avenge her by killing the monster that took her life. I know it was a supernatural creature that killed my aunt. Not some wild animals like police reports and autopsies say. I saw with my own two eyes who, or what, killed her."

Derek looked at me like there was something wrong with me. He looked at me with the most confusion I've ever seen from a guy's face.

"Ericka, I know that you're depressed and that

you're grieving the loss of your aunt. But I need to remind you that your aunt was mauled by a wild animal. It's dangerous to go out and search for some wild –"

"I'm not going insane."

"I know that –"

"No, you don't. You sound like everybody else who thinks I've gone off the rails. People think I'm crazy and I'm not. I know what I saw that night. I saw a shifting monster kill my aunt Carrie and it ate her heart right in front of me. I'm not delusional, I'm not out of touch with reality, I know what I saw."

"You're not making any sense, though. You're filled with trauma and grief. These things can cause you to say and do erratic things. You need to accept the fact that it was a wild animal that attacked and killed your aunt. The sooner you do, the sooner you'll hear from all of this."

My blood boiled to the highest of temperatures. I was like a volcano wanting to erupt and melt Derek with the lava of my words.

"I'll find my aunt's killer, with or without your help. I called you for help, but clearly you won't believe me or help me."

Derek lowered and shook his head while a look of pain and sadness overtook his face. But I wasn't going to give him the satisfaction of feeling like I was being too harsh on him. I was on a mission and he deserved every word I said for thinking that I was crazy. It was then that the opportunity to question Derek about his appearance in the forest that night came to me. It was a chance I was going to take advantage of to get answers from Derek about his true identity.

"You never quite told to me how you found me in the forest the night my aunt died, or why you were almost naked. Care to explain everything to me everything since we're alone right now?"

"What is there to explain? I was simply going for a swim at a nearby lake. It's that simple."

"You looked an awful lot dry for someone who had just finished swimming, though. In a lake, too, so I imagine you would've been extremely wet after swimming in a big body of water. It also doesn't explain why your shorts were torn up."

"Are you trying to accuse me of something?"

"No. I just want answers as to why you were suddenly there when I was being attacked by a shifting monster."

"Okay one, you weren't attacked by a 'shifting monster.' Two, while I was drying up after my swim, my shorts snagged on something and they got torn apart. Third, I heard noises and commotion in the forest coming from a wolf, which I think was the true killer of your aunt. I thought the wolf attacked you, too, so I came over to you to see how you were doing. That's all."

It's interesting you say 'wolf.' I never mentioned any wolves.

"See, here's the thing, though. That's not all. Because

I'm good at making connections. I don't appreciate why you're lying and saying that it was a wolf who murdered my aunt. I know what I saw. But I'm back to making connections."

I sat up on the bench and looked Derek square in the eyes, hoping to catch a glimmer of deception from him.

"You're right. I did see a wolf. But the wolf saved me from that monster. Since shifting monsters exist, I guess maybe *werewolves* must exist too, right? But the smoking gun evidence is the wolf's eyes. They match yours, and your sudden appearance in the forest that night can be explained by the fact that you, Derek, are the werewolf."

Derek sat up and looked at me with bulging, crazy eyes while his mouth wide open.

"Oh my gosh! What are you talking about, Ericka? Me? A werewolf? What is this, *Twilight*? I'm not a werewolf! For Pete's sake! Do you even hear yourself?"

"You're lying to me! I'll find ways to detect that you're a wolf. Maybe if I shoved a bunch of silver in your face, maybe you would turn into a wolf or something! And once I find out you're a wolf, I'll expose you to this town. That's it. I'm done with you and your friendship. Lose my number and don't contact me ever again!"

I was about to leave when Derek grabbed my arm and told me to wait. I pushed off of him, almost creating a scene in front of other park goers. He took a few steps back and motioned with hands for me to stop.

"Wait, wait! Okay, let me explain! You're right about everything. I was just afraid to confirm it to you. Please let me explain. I'm not a werewolf. But they do exist. Please, Ericka. I don't want to lose your friendship."

I could see tears starting to flow down Derek's face. I froze in my place and grew a worried look on my face. I sat down next to him on the bench and prepared myself for what he had to say. Derek wiped a few tears from his face and started talking.

"Werewolves exist. The monster that killed your aunt also exists. The proper term for them is shapeshifter. I believe you, Ericka. I'm sorry for lying and hiding it from you. Werewolves exist, shapeshifters exist, but they're not the only ones."

A look of surprise overcame my face, so much so that I covered my lips with the palms of my hand.

"What do you mean they're not the only ones?"

"You think this world is entirely human? Well, that's not true. Monsters exist and have been existent since the dawn of man. Werewolves and shapeshifters are only two races out of many that occupy this world."

"Care to list a few?" I said in a shocked manner.

"Witches, wizards…vampires…wendigos, and others out there, Ericka. I can't list them all."

I covered my mouth again to contain the shock that I felt. It vibrated throughout my body and I started to get goosebumps through every part of my skin. I could tell Derek was uncomfortable revealing the monsters he told me about, rubbing his head and eyes while avoiding contact with me.

"Vampires? Witches? What the fuck is a wendigo?"

"It doesn't matter, Ericka. I just hope that my admission makes you trust me again. Please, I just don't want to lose your friendship. I hope you forgive me for lying to you."

"If you're making admissions, then are you going to admit to me that you're the werewolf I saw that night?"

"No, because it wasn't me. I know the werewolf you saw."

"Know him? What does that mean?"

Derek huffed and placed his hands on his face, rubbing the last remaining tears until his cheeks were red. He took his hands off his face and turned to look at me.

"It's a childhood friend named Josh."

I maintained the look of shock on my face for longer. A friend of mine is also friends…with a monster? I didn't know if he was lying or telling the truth. I had to believe Derek for now because I didn't have any proof he was being deceptive.

"You're friends with a werewolf?"

"Yes. I was understanding towards him, Ericka. Josh is like a brother to me. I couldn't just abandon him because I've known him all my life."

"But aren't you afraid for your life?"

"No! He's never ever hurt me! I swear on my life!"

The look of surprise dissipated from my face. I couldn't *not* trust Derek from what he told me. Maybe he was telling the truth. After all, he was still alive so maybe Josh really never hurt him.

"How did Josh know where I was with the shapeshifter?"

"Werewolves have heightened senses of their surroundings. They also have really good noses and can smell something from fifty to a hundred feet away. It's part of their supernatural powers."

"How do you know so much about monsters and the supernatural?"

"Most of it came from a TV show I love watching. And there's Josh, too. Monsters know more about other monsters."

"What TV show?"

"It's called *Supernatural*. You've never heard of it."

I shook my head to answer Derek's question and told him that it wasn't the type of show I watched.

"It's alright. But I hope we're good, okay? Just let me know what I need to do to make it up to you. I don't want to lose you, Ericka. You're a very sweet person and I really don't want to lose you over this. Just please, I hope you can forgive me. I gave you all my honesty just now."

I nodded and looked on the ground. I considered Derek's plea for a moment before turning to face him again and nodding again.

"Yeah, we're good. I forgive you."

Derek got excited and donned a smile on his face. He wiped the last of his tears and embraced me, where

I felt his warmth again for a minute before he let me go.

"Thank you so much. You have no idea how much this means to me."

I, too, smiled at him, just not as enthusiastic as his.

"I'm sorry for making you cry. You are so sweet. I don't want to lose your friendship, either."

"Thank you. It means a lot...you know what, Ericka? Let's do this. I'm going to help you get revenge for your aunt. This is one way I'll make it up to you. I can't say no to you, so I'm in."

"Really? You're serious?"

"I am. I don't want you to go through this battle alone. You need backup. I'll also talk to Josh in case we need him again. I'll also teach you how to master a few weaponries. I'll train you to use a gun, a machete, and other weapons. That way you can kick some monster ass."

"Wow...Umm...well, how do you know how to use those things?"

"My dad used to hunt a lot, so he taught and trained me to defend myself, and to use those weapons."

I didn't know how to answer Derek. One minute he was lying to my face and thinking I was delusional. Now he wanted to help and believed me after he spilled his guts about the existence of monsters. It was after I threatened him with efforts to see if he was a wolf. Did he agree to help me get me off his back and forget about pursuing the truth if he's a wolf? Was there really a childhood friend named Josh?

I wanted to follow my instincts, but I had no evidence. I had to let this thing play out. I had to let him help me.

"Thanks. I don't know what to say other than thank you."

"You're welcome. The real thanks, though, is when we capture and kill the shifter who killed your aunt Carrie."

6

W*hat have you done, Derek, what have you done?*

Ericka is on to me. She's having her suspicions about me being the wolf who saved her. Now I'm screwed if I don't keep up with my lie and create a childhood friend out of thin air. I can't lose Ericka. She's just the most beautiful girl I've ever laid my eyes on. I mean, I have seen some beautiful girls in the past, but she takes the cake.

That day I saw her in the cafeteria at school was one of the most memorable days in my life. She was just all alone. This sweet, beautiful girl was all alone with no one to sit with, and I just had to meet her and sit with her to form our friendship. But now I have to fight like hell to keep Ericka in my life. I can't let her know about my true identity. I'll do whatever it takes to make sure I legitimize my lie and make it a reality so I don't lose the girl I may someday fall in love with.

I wasn't made a wolf. I was born one. I come from a long line of werewolves that have existed since the freakin' dawn of mankind. Werewolves all descended from the firstborn in the world, an alpha werewolf. My lineage contains a few pureblood werewolves who were born closer to the generation of the alpha. It's these pureblood werewolves who are leaders of packs throughout America and probably the world. There are no 'alphas' per se. Just pureblood wolves who were labeled alphas because of how old they were.

What I told Ericka was right. I came from the state of Washington and lived near Spokane, in Spokane Valley. I was naturally a part of my dad's pack since he was a pureblood wolf and the leader of a pack there. But I ran away from the pack when he was murdered. I quit the pack and ran away when I was ten years old.

My dad owned a cabin here in Wisconsin as a summer and winter vacation spot. I inherited it as part of his will and now it's my home. I paced throughout the entire living room looking for a way to make sure Ericka doesn't know about me. If there's even a snow-ball's chance that I can keep her in my life without her ever knowing who I was, I was taking it.

I was in the forest that night when she was attacked. I happened to be at the right place at the right time. I was taking a run in the forest out of boredom, and I was looking for something to eat for dinner. I was in the mood for some raw meat. That's when I started sniffing a human, but the scent was familiar to me. I smelled it that day in the cafeteria and recognized Ericka's smell. She was being chased by the shapeshifter and I just ran to her as fast as I could.

I credit my speed for getting there in time and saving her. I also credited my nose for alerting me to the fact that it was Ericka. She would've been dead meat and I wouldn't have gotten to know her. I wasn't lying to Ericka when I told her werewolves have heightened senses and noses strong enough to smell something fifty to a hundred feet away.

But now I'm wishing I had some shapeshifter powers because I wanted to change my appearance. The only way for Ericka to know my lie is true is for me to either assume an appearance or hire someone to pretend to be my childhood friend. I walked through the living room desiring the power to shapeshift so I can make 'Josh' exist. Either that or I can shop for a mask at a Halloween store.

I didn't have more time to think about the subject before I heard a knock on my cabin door. I also smelled two distinct stenches at the same time. Werewolves can detect others through our stench, and it was then that I know two wolves stood on the porch at my door. Not only that but we are able to know these scents for all our lives. I recognized these two distinct smells. They were two wolves that belonged in my dad's pack.

I went to the door and opened it, after which I saw the wolves were Chandler and Frank. They were two wolves I've known in the pack since I was nine. They were slightly older than me and I wasn't really close to them. We've only interacted like three times in my life.

Chandler was about my height while Frank was a little smaller. They both had black hair, but Frank grew a beard I hadn't seen before.

Both of them smiled slightly at me but I responded with a more serious look.

"Derek," Chandler said. "It's good to see you again. Long time no see."

"I assume you're here for news about my uncle."

"We are," Frank said. "We're here to let you know that per your request, your uncle's pack is now here. We all arrived a few nights ago but we would've been here sooner had we not been busy looking for a place to live in."

"Did you find it?"

"No. We just set up some yurts out in a field outside the forest, away from civilians," Chandler replied.

"We would have asked you if we could set them up closer to your cabin or even squat here for a few days in your cabin," Frank said. "But your uncle chose not to do that given how you feel about him."

I closed my eyes in irritation as I remembered truly how I felt towards my uncle. I balled up my fists as I tried to pacify all the anger with me towards him for what he did. I opened my eyes again and I looked at Chandler and Frank.

"You didn't need to remind me."

"Anyways, we just thought we would drop by and let you know your uncle and the pack are all here. He hopes to meet with you soon and talk to you. He hasn't seen you for years."

"I'll decide when I see my uncle."

"Fine," Chandler said. "Have it your way. Consider the message delivered. Come on, Frank. We'll catch you later, Derek."

The two wolves walked away from the door and into the darkness of the forest. I closed the door so loud behind them that they probably heard the bang from their location in the forest. Werewolf noses weren't the only thing heightened. We could even hear a fly when it lands on our fur.

I tried to get Uncle Jason out of my head. But Chandler and Frank's visit reminded me of the horrible crime he did – the death of my father. The rifle bullet in my father Matthew's heart came from him. He claimed it was an accident when they were hunting one night. He became pack alpha after my dad died, which made me believe to be the reason he killed my father.

But my uncle denied that and spent so many nights begging for forgiveness from my mom and me. I was too angry and grief-struck to believe him. I was still full of anger and hatred towards him. There was no way I would look past it or even hear his defense. And yet, he was here because I wanted him to be. I requested that he be here. I just hope I don't regret it.

7

I haven't been to my dad's storage unit in almost two decades. I imagined that all of his stuff and some of my mom's stuff stored there would be covered with so much dust and mold. But I wasn't going there for the junk. I was going to daddy's storage unit for the weapons he owned when he was alive. I was going to take Derek up on his offer to train me in weapon use, but I didn't have my own weapons.

Derek and I did have a lot in common. Our fathers were both hunters, but my dad quit hunting around the time I was born. It wasn't a major hobby of his and he saw it as a distraction from his 'new family.' He didn't fathom me ever taking up hunting like him, but he didn't know about monsters. His little girl hadn't entered the world of the supernatural yet. If only he knew.

I got to the facility and walked down the hall to my dad's unit on the left end of the hall. I unlocked the storage unit with the key to the disc lock that was entrusted to my aunt by my mother. I slid the door up and saw many boxes of junk in front of me. Dust particles swarmed me and the air of the unit, and I swiped my hands in the air to clear the dust away from me.

I walked over to a few boxes surrounded by a family of dust bunnies. I opened one of them and saw a silver handgun with a bunch of rusty, withered bullets right next to them. But I was shocked when I saw a trio of arrows leaning against one corner of the box. I looked for a bow in the storge space but couldn't find it.

It was then that I picked the box up and placed it on the side before I opened the box underneath. It was inside this box that I found the bow, which was blackish gray in color. It sat right next to a crossbow in the same color. I picked up the bow and the crossbow. The strings on them were fragile and I saw some cracks on both of them. They weren't functional anymore.

Ugh.

I placed the weapons back in the box and closed it before putting the other box on top of it. I then walked to my right and saw a third box on the floor leaning against the back wall. I opened it up and saw only one thing in there: a stainless-steel machete with a black plastic handle.

I picked the machete up with both my hands and examined it in the dark lit light. I swiped some of the dust that was covering it off. It was still good to use, and I decided to take it home with me. I left the storage unit and locked the disc lock. I took my phone out and dialed Derek's number and put it up to my ear.

"Hello?" Derek said.

"Hey, it's Ericka. I went to my dad's old storage store because I don't own any weapons, so I found this machete we can use. Do you have anything we can use for me to train with?"

"Yeah, of course I do. We can start today instead of tomorrow like we agreed on if you want. You can come over to the cabin right now."

"Really? Wow, thanks. I'm coming over now."

"Great! See you soon!"

"You, too."

———

Derek and I were in the very large backyard behind his cabin, and we stood in front of a tree stump where he put a gun, a bow and arrow, and my dad's machete. He installed five scarecrows in front of us that he made from a long pole and a bunch of hay a couple of days ago in preparation for my training. He told me he purchased the hay online and it came the next day.

Derek picked the gun up and held it with both arms before aiming at the scarecrow to the left of the one in the middle. He had me wear earplugs and a pair of goggles when I came to the cabin. He fired two bullets at the scarecrow, one hitting its chest, the other in the forehead. He turned to look at me.

"Alright, it's your turn. Ready?"

"I think so. I don't know why I'm nervous, though."

"You'll be fine. Here."

Derek reached his hand out to me with the gun so I could take it. I held it with my right hand and Derek took my other one to place it on the grip.

"Alright, hold it with both your hands and aim at the scarecrow. Aim anywhere on its body or head. You got this."

"Okay."

I aimed the gun at the scarecrow with my fingers sweating and shaking. I pressed the trigger and the recoil of the gun sent me back a few steps while the bullet zipped past one of the scarecrow's shoulder into the forest. I shook my head in agitation as Derek came up to me.

"Ericka, it's okay, don't worry. That's why we practice. Try again, alright? And don't be discouraged."

"Okay. You're right."

"Just grip the gun real hard in your hand and secure yourself in your position so you don't get knocked back by the recoil."

"Sounds good."

I took aim at the scarecrow again, securing myself in a position like Derek advised. I aimed the barrel at the chest and fired one more bullet. I didn't jerk back to life before and I hit the target on its shoulder. It wasn't what I aimed for but it was encouraging to see I didn't miss. I looked at Derek and I saw him nodding and smiling at me.

"That was much better. Let's try a few more shots."

"Alright."

I aimed the gun back at the scarecrow and fired two more bullets. With no recoil, the first bullet struck its stomach while the second bullet pierced its heart.

"Yes! Making progress!" I heard Derek shout.

I looked at him with a satisfactory smile on my face.

"Thanks, Derek. I appreciate the encouragement."

"Alright, let's get back to shooting later. Let's work on using the machete right now."

I walked up the stump and took my dad's machete in my hands. Derek walked up to me and placed his hands on top of mine.

"Alright, we need to work on your grip because you're going to be swinging this thing around with only one hand."

Derek showed me how to handle the machete by securing it tight in his palm. We both walked up to the nearest scarecrow and Derek made a pair of wild swings at its chest. He made it look so easy with the blade gripped tight in his massive hands. Derek walked up to me and reached his hand out for me to take the blade.

"Your turn."

I took the blade from Derek and held it with one hand, squeezing the handle snug to my palm. I walked up to the scarecrow and swung at it once before the blade got stuck in the scarecrow's chest. Derek couldn't help but snicker a little at my mistake before going up to the scarecrow and getting the blade unstuck.

"You just need to swing at it, not stab it. It's okay, though. Don't be discouraged. You'll make progress."

I couldn't help but feel that way. But I took the blade from Derek's hands and tried again. I swung two furious times at the scarecrow and slashed it in its chest and stomach.

"Much better," Derek said. "Let's do it a few more times. Swing as many times at it as possible until you feel confident. The key is to let the blade touch the skin but not enough to penetrate it. I'll teach you that later on."

I nodded and aimed the machete up at the scarecrow. I did as Derek said and slashed it so many times, I couldn't keep count. I did much better this round as I saw with gratification the massive number of indents and diagonal lines on the torso of the scarecrow.

"Alright, that's enough machete for today. How do you feel?"

"Good. Really good. Thank you so much for helping me do this."

I walked up to Derek and gave him a hug of appreciation. He hugged me back and I felt the warmth of his large body up against mine. I couldn't help but sigh over how tight he wrapped himself around me. I was sweating a little bit but I didn't care if it touched his skin. I just wrapped my arms around him because of how happy I felt.

"It's my pleasure. I'm happy to help. What do you say we work on the bow and arrow now?"

I let go of Derek and groaned a little bit.

"Why do we have to work on that? I'm satisfied with just using the machete and the gun. I feel like the bow and arrow is complicated."

"What are you worried about? You have the best instructor in the world with you. Don't fret a thing. Come on, let's give it a try."

Derek and I walked over to the stump and he picked up the bow and arrow. He placed the arrow on the bow and stood a far distance, about twenty feet away from the scarecrow in the middle of the other one. He stood upright with his feet and shoulders apart at a certain angle. Derek aimed the bow and arrow at the scarecrow and drew back the string. He released the arrow and it shot straight into the middle torso of the scarecrow. It was a sight that made me jump a little and I looked at Derek with my eyes and lips wide open.

"You expect me to do that?"

"Relax! I'll teach you. There's nothing to it."

Easy for you to say!

Derek motioned for me to come to him, and I walked over to where he was. He took my hands and placed the bow and arrow in them.

"It's your turn now."

"Maybe I shouldn't –"

"Relax. You can trust me, alright?"

"Okay."

Derek walked behind me and took my hands with the bow and arrow in his. I felt his body lean against my back, a sensation that sent shivers all over my nerves. He showed me how to place the arrow on the bow and how to hold it in front of me. Derek had me stand at the same angle he stood at just a few minutes ago.

"You need to have a relaxed grip on the bow. Place the arrow on the shelf here, position your index finger above the arrow and two fingers below. Draw the string to the point where your pulling hand is under your chin."

Derek adjusted the aim of the bow with my hands so that it's targeted at the scarecrow. He came behind me again and gripped my hands in his. He helped me release the arrow and it landed underneath the arrow he shot earlier in the torso of the scarecrow.

"That's how you do it."

"Oh my gosh, that was so cool and exciting!"

"With time, you'll be doing that yourself. But I think that's enough for today. We'll be back at it tomorrow afternoon, alright?"

"Sounds good!"

8

I was at the local library trying to do research on shapeshifters in my goal to find and kill the one who took my aunt's life. I was supposed to meet Derek to work on this, but he wasn't here yet. He told me he had to take care of some work for school and run errands for the cabin. I thought about what Derek told me about monsters as I took in the smell of the musty books that occupied dozens of shelf space in the cases in front of me.

My nose also picked up the scent of the mahogany wood of the bookcases. The two odors were combatting the scent of a fragrance plugin hidden somewhere in the library, which smelled like spiced apple or some type of citrusy fruit. It was a battle for smell supremacy that distracted me from my train of thought.

Back to Derek, girl.

I took some time to reflect about what Derek told

me about monsters. I focused more specifically on the existence of shapeshifters and werewolves. Josh then came to mind, the supposed wolf who saved me from the shapeshifter that awful night. I couldn't help but sense alarm bells blaring in my head and getting a knot in my stomach. Something was wrong. I think Derek lied to me.

It didn't make sense to me why his friend Josh saved me that night. If Josh existed, and that's a big 'if' because the basis of my instincts is that Josh wasn't real, why did he find me and attack the shapeshifter? He didn't know me and I sure as hell didn't know him. I didn't believe that a random ass wolf would be in the forest to save me when it never met me. I found it hard to believe that "Josh the Werewolf" was in the forest and had a strong smell that determined my location.

Something in my intuition told me that there was something off about Derek's story. I think he was involved in my rescue. If it wasn't him who was the werewolf and it was indeed this Josh guy, I think Derek somehow knew my location and told his friend where I was at so he could rescue me. Either way, Derek was involved, and I don't appreciate being lied to right in my face.

There were other details I glossed over that suddenly came to my mind while I was doing my research or trying to. This train of thought distracted me from my mission severely. Derek and the werewolf had the same eye color. Did Josh have bright green eyes too? I needed to remind myself to ask Derek if Josh's eyes were green, too. Of course, he could say yes and end up lying to me. I just needed to find evidence to prove this mass deception within Derek existed.

Second, didn't monsters have inhuman minds of their own? Why did Josh, a werewolf, save me from another monster? He was a monster too, so monsters should have minds of their own in their true form. Josh could've killed me and finished the job that the shapeshifter started with my aunt. Instead, he spared my life for some reason.

Unless it wasn't 'Josh.'

There were too many inconsistencies to count. They were giving me a fucking headache. I was too distracted from doing research in the library. I leaned back against my very uncomfortable hardwood chair and stretched my back and body. I rubbing my eyes and forehead to reconcentrate on what I was doing.

My heart and intuition told me that Derek was the werewolf. He just didn't want to scare me so I would stop being his friend. Or maybe his intentions were more than friendship. I don't know. All I knew was, I couldn't fathom being friends with or associated with a monster like Derek was with 'Josh.'

I needed solid evidence to finally determine if the person who I deemed a friend of mine was one of the many dangerous monster races out there. My life was on the line. Maybe if I caught him transforming into a wolf on a full moon. I could maybe stalk Derek one night on a full moon to see if he changes into his true form.

But it had to wait. I had to refocus back onto my main mission. The screen of my computer was locked on the Google search bar and its white background. I typed the word "shapeshifter" into the search bar. A large list of results popped up nanoseconds later on the screen, all of which were an irrelevant disappointment.

I put my face into the palms of my hands when I found page after page of shapeshifters in fiction and mythology. I also found several episode articles about shapeshifters in Derek's favorite TV show *Supernatural*. I found nothing about shapeshifters in real life. I was annoyed as fuck, but it didn't prevent me from trying again.

I tried a different approach. I typed up several keyword strings into the search bar. "Shapeshifters in real life" was one of them. 'Shapeshifter strengths and weaknesses" was another. I knew I hit a dead end on both keyword strings when the first result of the first page was the wiki page of *Supernatural* listing the strengths and weaknesses of shapeshifters.

My frustration reached a peak point. I clicked ferociously out of the Google site in anger while my face got blood red. The visible look of anger on my face was observed by other library goers sitting near me. Some of the library staff working on shelves near where I sat also saw how upset I was. It was only for a split second, though, and they went back to work when I shot them all angry looks.

An idea popped into my head after this miniature episode of temper. I was really stupid for not thinking about it earlier. I was in a damn library. It was the internet before the internet existed. Since this 21st century crap didn't help, I figured maybe there was a book of non-fiction here on monsters that would help me in my desperate search for any answers.

I huffed and released a sigh of stress. I got up from my chair, feeling sore in my lower back area and my upper butt cheeks. I stretched from side to side while other people working near my table looked at me for a brief second. They wanted to see what the wild movements they saw from the corners of their crusty red eyes were and where they came from before returning to work.

I wasted valuable time on Google when I could've used that time wisely by scouring the library for something useful. There were a gazillion books here on every topic fathomable to humans. There must be something about monsters and the supernatural here. I hurried to the non-fiction section of the library with no time to waste.

I looked at shelf after shelf of books in numerous categories: photography, biographies and memoirs, humor and entertainment, cookbooks and food, health and fitness, religion, parenting, sports and outdoors… the list goes on. There was no whiff of anything about the supernatural. Nothing at all. It was all in the fiction section, in books with plots about girls falling in love with monsters, monster hunters, etc.

Fuck my life.

I couldn't find any books about monsters or how to kill them. I felt like an utter failure, lost in a maze made out of haystacks in which I was trying to find a golden needle. Oh, and while unicycling and trying to catch lightning in a bottle. It was impossible and entirely hopeless. I couldn't help but feel my emotions welling up inside me.

My heart felt like a sponge filled with water, waiting to release some of the soaked-up tears I gathered from the tragic, unfortunate events in my life. I could feel some of those tears rising up to the lids of my eyes and I immediately tried to clear them before anybody could see me. I rushed over to my laptop and grabbed it along with my other belongings. I placed everything inside my backpack before any more tears welled up in my eyes.

I hurried to the exits of the library before anybody could see the tears forming in my eyes. It didn't take long for me to find my blue Nissan Altima and I unlocked it while I was about twenty feet from it. I swung the door open once I got to the car and slammed my backpack with my precious little laptop into the passenger side. I plopped into the driver seat before slamming the door extra hard.

I planted my face into the steering wheel and released the long-awaited tears that my spongy heart soaked up. It felt good to release all those built-up tears once I was alone in the comfort of my car's leather seats. It was like when I would go to the bathroom in an emergency and release all the urine that's been held there. It felt good to release all that anguish from off my chest.

I didn't take comfort in crying for too long as I heard a knocking on the window.

"Ericka?"

Ahh, now that's a voice I'm familiar with.

Derek's voice vibrated in the air because of the way it carried through the window. I took my face off the wheel and began to wipe as many tears as possible, so Derek doesn't see me in such an emotional wreck. Although he may have already heard me cry every ounce of frustration and misery so it may have been too late.

I took control of myself and kept whatever tears left in me in check before I could look at Derek through my window. I could see the painful look of concern on his face when he looked into my eyes and saw just how watery they were. I rolled the window down and wiped my runny nose.

"Hey, Derek."

"Are you alright? What happened?"

"I'll explain to you everything. Just get in the car."

Derek scurried to the passenger seat and I unlocked the door for him. Once he got into the car, he wrapped his arms around me and pulled me against him before I could say anything. I wanted to pull away based on all the suspicions I had about him. I wanted to cut to the chase with everything that's happened and just interrogate the shit out of him to get the information I wanted. But…

I couldn't do it. His large stature provided me with so much warmth and comfort. He provided me with a shoulder to lean on and cry on. I wrapped my arms around his shoulder blades and once again started to be consumed with emotions. It was like Derek let me know it's alright to lean on him and release all my feelings and emotions to him by hugging me. He was like a support system that I badly needed right now because I felt so lost, confused, and filled with frustration and rage.

Derek finally let go of me and wiped some tears from under my eyes. I could see the extremely worried look on his face as he started to rub my back with his outsized hand.

"I'm so sorry for not being here sooner. I'm so angry at myself right now. I feel like a douche, Ericka, I'm so sorry."

"It's okay. Thanks for the hug. I sort of needed it."

Derek nodded and donned a lukewarm smile on his face.

"Where were you?"

"I was doing homework at the cabin and I had to go to the grocery store to fill up the kitchen. On my way over here, there was a lot of traffic and I couldn't get here fast enough. I was about to go inside the library when I saw you here."

I looked down at the steering wheel and started to wipe it from all the tears and snot that flowed from my face. I nodded about what Derek told me, seeing there was no way not to believe him. It's not like I had any evidence to prove he was lying about where he was. But I was waiting on other crucial pieces of evidence to back up what my guts felt.

I looked up at Derek and saw that he maintained the same puppy look of concern on his face for me.

"I'm so sorry for not being here earlier."

"It's okay. You don't have to keep apologizing. I understand."

"Tell me what happened. Why are you crying so much?"

I sighed and looked at Derek's bright green eyes, the same eyes that laid the foundation of my instincts about his true identity. I rattled with nervousness when I looked into those eyes, but I managed to calm my nerves and before I knew it, my lips parted.

"I was in the library doing research about shapeshifters and how to kill them, but I couldn't find them on the stupid fucking internet. So, I tried to find any book in the library about the supernatural world and monsters to see if maybe there was something in there about shapeshifters. I hit a dead end and I basically ran out of the library trying not to cry until I came here. I tried so many damn keywords, but nothing came up except results about that stupid show you watch. It seems like everything about monsters is fiction, but I know what I saw."

I observed Derek bow his head down and start to rub the back of his neck. He maintained that same worried look on his face and then bobbed his head back up to face me.

"What? Derek? Is there something you have to say?"

"Yes. Every result you found about monsters is fiction because it's fiction to the human world. Had I been here earlier, I would have warned you about that. But basically, everything regarding monsters is mere fiction to humans. But you and I are not just any human. We have knowledge about monsters and there's only one source of information that will reveal all the answers you're looking for."

A look of shock formed on my face.

So, I wasn't stupid.

"One source? Where is it? What is it?"

"Before I tell you what it is, I need to reveal to you a little story."

I sat up in the driver seat in anticipation because I knew Derek was going to lay some deep revelations on me. I needed to brace myself and I did. With all my attention on Derek and my wide eyes looking at him, I began to listen to what he said.

"There was a legendary hunter by the name of Bartholomew Ramsey who lived in the 1800s, but he went by the nickname Bart. Bart is said to have killed every monster of each race on this planet, including shapeshifters. Bart never shared his knowledge of monsters and how to kill them to maintain their existence a secret."

The surprised look on my face grew as I continued listening to Derek.

"But towards the end of his life, he did write all of his knowledge about every monster race and how to slay them inside a book, which he entrusted to a good friend of his, who happened to be a witch."

"Holy shit, are you serious?"

"Yes. Why would I be telling you this story if I was bullshitting you? I'd be wasting your time."

"Ugh, just get to the good part already."

"Bart died in 1874. Ever since his death, no one has known the whereabouts of this book except for his witch friend."

I placed my hands on my lips. A muffled "Oh my gosh!" came out, to which Derek replied by nodding.

"That's why you couldn't find anything on monsters in the library or the internet. Because all the knowledge about monsters and how to kill them is inside Bart's book, and it simply doesn't exist in the human world."

"How do you know about Bart Ramsay and his book?"

"Josh told me. Like I said, only monsters know about the existence of this book. Every monster race in America has been trying to find this book to destroy it and its knowledge, but obviously they failed."

I sat back in my chair and rubbed my brain to grasp what Derek told me. I turned back to him and looked at his green eyes.

"How the hell are we supposed to find this book?"

"We need a plan. But first, we need to weaken this shapeshifter."

"Any ideas?"

"From what Josh told me, shapeshifters are weakened by silver and iridium. So, we need to gather weapons made out of those things and use them against the shifters. Also, I had this idea that maybe you can wear this silver necklace so the shifter can't come near you or touch you without being weakened by the necklace."

I nodded my head and managed a mild smile. Despite my suspicions about him, Derek made me smile and it was something I could use right now.

"Sounds like a good idea. But we need to talk about something before you leave."

Derek turned his entire body towards me and perked up his ears. I was going to take this opportunity to get some things off my chest, since I had Derek all to myself in my car.

"I should've said some*one*. It's Josh."

"What about him?"

"When can I meet this friend of yours? Where does he even live?"

"He's not exactly a people person. He lives in an isolated cabin of his own, not too far from mine. I talked to him about it but he flat-out refused because he feared you would tell the public and cause a scare in the town. He didn't want to be exposed and hunted down."

I opened my lips to the fullest extent, wanting to say something at that moment but it didn't come out until seconds later.

"It sounds like you're describing yourself. You remember when I threatened to find a way to expose you as a wolf when you didn't believe me about my aunt's death?"

"Yes, and I was beginning to forget about it until you just brought it up. Josh is the wolf, not me. But you need me to promise me something."

"What's that?"

"You can't tell a living soul, a living *human* soul about Josh's existence as a werewolf. You need to promise me that you'll keep everything you know a secret. Please, Ericka. You have to. He's my best friend. He saved you from that shifter, so the least you could do is keep it a secret. I don't want my best friend to be hunted down and dead."

I huffed and nodded, looking down at my steering wheel before looking at Derek again.

"I promise not to tell anybody. You have my word."

I was back in the forest behind Derek's cabin with him and the same setup in front of us. Derek had me grip the gun with only one hand today and I shot so many missing bullets that I just felt like giving up and not using a gun anymore.

"Come on, Ericka. Don't beat yourself up over it too much. It's okay if you miss it. You're in the second day of training."

"I just don't know why I feel so weak and horrible, then!"

"You're none of those things! Just keep trying! Grip the gun with confidence and aim at the target with ease. You can do this."

I did what Derek advised and took a tighter grip on the gun. I aimed at a scarecrow to my right using my dominant eye. I pressed the trigger, and it went straight into the stomach of the scarecrow, an effort that impressed me after a mostly difficult day.

"There you go! You got it!"

I shot a few more rounds at the scarecrow and all of them landed in its torso. It was then that I learned the keys to using a gun for me were to grip the gun with confidence and use my dominant eye for better aiming. I felt like I mastered the gun today, after which Derek and I moved onto the machete.

I gripped the machete in one hand and tried to slash at the scarecrow, but the blade got stuck on it again. I wanted to feel discouraged so bad, but I looked at Derek and he gave me a small smile of encouragement to keep going. I pried the machete off the scarecrow and tried again, more determined than before.

I gripped the handle of the machete better and tighter while I readjusted my back muscles. I figured I would get much of my energy and accuracy from the muscles in my back, and I re-aimed the machete at the scarecrow. With more confidence streaming through my veins and gathering all my power and strength from my shoulders and back muscles, I slashed so many times at the scarecrow and they all landed on its torso.

"Yes! You got it, Ericka!"

I was so proud of myself for all the hard work I put in to master the machete with one hand. Derek's encouraging words and excitement also made me feel really good about myself, as I felt like the sweat, I shed was well worth it.

"So, I have good news for you."

"What is it?"

"We won't practice the bow and arrow today!"

"Yes!" I said with a fist pump.

"But we are practicing something else."

The excitement had disappeared. I was afraid it was something harder than a bow and arrow, like an ax or a sword, or maybe even a flamethrower.

"Oh gosh, what is it?"

"Follow me."

Derek started walking back to the cabin and I followed him with uneasy steps. He walked to the outside cellar door and unlocked it with a key from his pocket. Derek opened the cellar and motioned for me to come into it. I walked up to the door and saw a few steps. I walked down the steps and was greeted by a blue punching bag along with a pair of boxing pads and two pairs of boxing gloves.

"What is this?"

"We're going to learn something that'll substitute a bow and arrow – hand-to-hand combat."

"Really?"

"Really."

I got a little happy and excited as Derek put the boxing pads on. He tossed me the boxing gloves, which were also blue.

"Put those on and let's begin."

I did as Derek told me and I put the boxing gloves on, feeling their snug warm texture against the palms of my hands. I walked up to Derek and he put both of his hands up with the pads facing me.

"I want you to punch these pads as many times as you can and as hard as you can, too. The more you punch the pads, the more you'll get used to throwing punches in general. I want you to be very aggressive. Think about all the tragedy you've faced and think about everything bad that's happened in your life. Release all that stress and anger with every hit, okay? Let's do this."

I prepared to punch the pads had Derek had up. I jabbed each pad with as much fury and aggression Derek wanted, fueled by the thoughts of my mom and aunt's deaths, but more my aunt's death. Derek's hands were bouncing back as I hit the pads with all my might while my mind was churning with memories of that fateful night and my aunt's body in front of me...the shapeshifter in front of me eating my aunt's heart.

"Good, Ericka, good! Keep going!"

I felt sweat drip down my forehead as I kept punching Derek's pads. But I soon lost my energy and I stopped throwing any strikes. I leaned down and grabbed my thighs, inhaling and exhaling so much.

Derek leaned down to look at me with a big smile on his face.

"You did very good today, Ericka. I'm really proud of you."

"Thank you. I appreciate it."

9

I t was four in the afternoon and I started my third day of training with Derek in the cellar. We planned the session at four because Derek had school and homework to do. I started off the day throwing strikes at the pads Derek wore before he had me practice on the punching bag. I landed several kicks and strikes at the bag for twenty minutes, taking a couple of breaks in between.

Derek and I moved on to weaponry practice after the hand-to-hand combat session was done and we started off with the bow and arrow.

"Remember, stand upright, place the arrow on the shelf of the bow, pull the string back with the back muscles, and aim with your dominant eye before releasing. It's sort of like the gun and the machete. You can do this."

I nodded at Derek before turning my attention back to the bow and arrow. I concentrated my efforts on aiming using my right eye. I took my eye off the target to make sure that the arrow was secure on the shelf and the string was tightly drawn. I then went back to aiming with my dominant eye and released the arrow. I was ecstatic when it hit the torso of the middle scarecrow and it encouraged me to do two more arrows.

Once I shot the two arrows in the same place, Derek was confident that I mastered the bow and arrow like I mastered the other two weapons. We spent the rest of the training session on the gun and the machete before calling it a day.

"I'm beyond proud of you for working so hard today despite feeling discouraged at times."

"I couldn't have done it without you. Thank you so much, Derek. You have no idea how much I appreciate you."

I wrapped my arms around him and snuggled tight against rock-solid torso and abs. Derek hugged me back and grabbed the lower end of my hair and my upper back. We stayed like this for a few minutes as the breeze of the day brushed against us.

It was eight in the evening and I was feeling comfortable in the confines of my bedroom in the Devereaux house. Even though I was hellbent on justice for my aunt, I still had a separate life from that to live. Now that I was living with my new family in their house, I needed to make myself useful. I needed a job soon.

I was on my laptop browsing online job boards looking for a job. I didn't know when I was going back to school after the events that unfolded with my aunt. It was already a struggle to go back to school for my senior year after the death of my mom, who died of a simple heart attack. My aunt had her heart ripped out of her chest. I didn't know when, or even if, I was going back to school to finish my senior year.

I was looking for a job to balance my life with my pursuit of revenge against that damn shapeshifter. I never balanced anything at once in my life. It was worth a try, though, especially if I needed a cover story to give the Devereauxs when they asked for my where-abouts when I went on long nights with Derek to hunt for the shapeshifter.

I weighed the risks in my mind of balancing a job with my secret mission. I had to brace myself for what-ever challenges I would face on this journey of mine of juggling two things at once. For one, I wouldn't see my best friend, practically my sister, for the majority of time while I have a job and hunt the shapeshifter down. Two, the job could possibly interfere with my secret plot of revenge if I had a night shift or something.

But there were other reasons I needed a job. I felt the stinging feeling of being a freeloader while I lived with the Devereauxs. They provided me with food and a roof over me after I was left homeless from my aunt's death. I had to repay them the favor. I had a plan in mind to rent a one-bedroom or studio apartment when I turned eighteen. I needed to save a boatload of money to do this, a goal that would take a while to achieve.

I also felt extremely horrible that MacKayla was paying for my car insurance and monthly payments. I adamantly rejected her doing that in the first place, telling her how much guilt I would carry on my shoulders if she did that. MacKayla wouldn't hear a word I had to say. She insisted on doing this for me, telling me that we were practically sisters and that I've been through enough sorrow in my life.

MacKayla wanted to help me in my life. She added that since her parents were working to support the house along with her brother Russell, she told me that her money was gathering cyber dust in her bank account. MacKayla wasn't a thrifty spender like most girls. She was the opposite and only purchased something when it was necessary.

I relented in the end, but I proposed a compromise with MacKayla. I told her that once I got a job, I would split the payments with her in my car. I would pay the bigger monthly payments and she would pay the smaller fee of my car insurance. But MacKayla scoffed at the compromise.

"I might as well just let you pay for everything for your car! All my money would have gone for nothing. It would defeat the purpose of why I gave you money in the first place. Besides, how are you going to save enough money for your apartment?"

MacKayla came up with a compromise of her own.

Even when I get a job, she would continue paying for my car and suggested I save up all my money for the studio or one-bedroom apartment, since I told her about it. By that point, I got bored with the debate and wanted to tap out so bad. I gave in to her compromise and we ended our quarrel with her compromise, which made MacKayla giddy with joy.

I just wanted to get a job to not feel useless in general. While Derek and I worked on my mission to get justice for my aunt, I still had a life to live, and I needed something to distract me during the time I wasn't looking for a way to kill that SOB shifter. I found so many jobs in one job board that I practically didn't need to go to any other one.

There were so many jobs that I could apply for that I practically made it a goal to apply to five of them a day in the hopes of getting one of them. Even if I didn't finish my education and obtain my GED, there were still options out there for me. I could be a warehouse worker, a server in a restaurant, a coffee barista, delivery driver, and so much more.

I applied to five jobs before calling it quits for the night. My eyes began to dry up and get red from looking at all the job listings. I rubbed my eyes at the same time I closed my laptop. If I looked at the screen one more time, I would need eye drops. I plopped down on my bed and stretched my body to loosen up all the sore muscles in my body.

I came up with an idea for the next thing I could do as soon as my head hit the pillow. I was bored out of my mind, so I decided to do some research on Bart Ramsay as some sort of validation on Derek's story. I typed "Bartholomew Ramsey" in the search bar. A multitude of pictures came straight into my face of the same artist sketch of a man with white hair and a white beard sitting in a chair holding a cane. The background was some white wall with nothing on it, not even pictures or any designs and decors.

No camera portraits of Bart existed. Only several takes of the same drawing of Bart by some anonymous artist filled the internet and I wondered why. I saw many articles about Bart, ranging from his adventures of monster hunting and how his *character* has redefined the horror and dark fantasy genres to the identity of the anonymous 'author' of the 'Bart Ramsey series' is.

It was then that I knew each and every article about Bart had something in common: they portrayed him as a fictional character instead of a real person. Derek's claim about the monster world and the supernatural being secret held true. I found a Wikipedia page on Bart and clicked on it.

The same illustration that I saw earlier, that so many later artists used for their own copycat styles and redesigns, was the same picture that adorned the top of the Wikipedia page for Bart. The page explained that Bart was a character in a fictional dark fantasy series, in which he is the protagonist bounty hunter noted for his many supernatural conquests of various monsters.

The author was anonymous, and the series is described as one of the earliest dark fantasy works in

America... He wanted his identity protected and the secret about monsters maintained. But who the hell was the author? Why reveal Bart's existence at all, let alone as some kind of fictitious character? If the purpose was to keep him and his monster hunting under wraps, who would uncover his identity for all of America to know?

My mind raced back to the conversation Derek and I had outside the library. I remembered him telling me about how Bart wrote about all of his hunts, the monsters he killed, and how he killed them along with their weaknesses in a book. The location of the book is unknown and the only one who knows about it is a witch who befriended the hunter.

The witch...*That's it!*

The author of "Anonymous" was not anonymous to me anymore. But why would the witch who Bart entrusted his book with write a series about him or expose him to everyone like that? Why would she detail his monster hunts in a fictional dark fantasy series? Did she decide to profit off Bart and his adventures because she was broke?

These questions swirled in my mind for a few seconds before a crucial epiphany came to my mind. If the witch wrote this series of dark fantasy books based on Bart and his monster hunts, and she used Bart's book as her number one source, what if I found and read the entire series to uncover the answers I needed to kill a shapeshifter?

That's it, girl! All you have to do is find the book in the series involving shapeshifters and read it. Then you'll know what to do to avenge your aunt!

My fingers tapped on the touchscreen of my phone with speed, searching for this series that the witch published about Bart. My spirit, however, was crushed when I found out that the series about Bart was no longer in print and had been out of print since the 1930s. I guess the popularity of the series fell to the point where there was no longer a reason to keep it in circulation.

Fuck!

I hoped to use this series as an alternative to Bart's book since only the witch, and God, knew where it was. I wanted to make my life easier and just read this series for answers. But I guess justice was taking me on the hard road to achieving it, not wanting me to take shortcuts or cut corners.

At least this research I did made me trust Derek more. He was being truthful about Bart and not just telling me a story to get me off his back about my suspicions. My instincts were roaring, and my intuition was howling as loud as Josh was when he saved me that night…if it was indeed Josh.

I couldn't go up against any monster without Derek's help, because he had a werewolf as one of his buddies. I knew I needed his help to avenge Aunt Carrie's death and it was crucial to find the shapeshifter and kill it with Josh's help. Besides, I could use Derek's knowledge about the supernatural. I wouldn't have known the first step to defeating the shapeshifter was to weaken it with silver until Derek and I found out what truly kills them.

I felt comfortable working with Derek on this. But I wasn't going to let my guard down around him. If I smell any whiff of deception or find any evidence that supported my instincts, I will come after him.

10

My body was enjoying the deep slumber. My eyes were tight shut, and I was in the middle of one of the best sleeps I've ever taken in my life. But I woke up to the loud text message notification sound of my phone. It sounded off twice, notifying me that I had two text messages to look at.

I reached for the phone on the dresser to the left side of my bed. My eyes were still shut as the sun shined through the window and right into my eyelids. I groaned heavily while I tried to open them. It was like they were sewn shut. I managed to slightly open them and reached for my phone.

I expected to have the phone in my hands, but my fingers accidentally pushed the phone off the dresser. I groaned even harder than the last time as I forced myself to open my eyes and fully wake up. I sighed as I stretched every part of my body. I extended my arms upwards while intertwining them together and pushing them towards the ceiling.

I stretched my legs outwards towards the bed post. I wound up overstretching them and felt the wrath of a ruthless cramp. I struggled to contain myself as the pain from the pulled muscle in my calf made me squirm in bed, trying to get this pain out of my leg. Once the Charley Horse was gone, I got out of bed and hobbled to my phone.

I still felt the pain of the cramp as I bent over and picked up my phone. I saw on the lock screen that there were two messages from Derek. My throat gave out a moan of annoyance as I reminded myself to voice my irritation with Derek the next time I see him. It was one of the most peaceful sleeps I've had, and he ruined it.

I opened my phone and went to the text message app. I opened the new messages with a furious tap of my finger, annoyed at Derek for waking me up and indirectly causing a cramp in my calf.

Derek: Hey, Ericka. I don't know if you're asleep or not, but I just wanted to text you and ask you if you're up for a game of bowling today.

Derek: We didn't get to do it before since...you know, happened. So, I was hoping that, if you're not doing anything today, we could go bowling? What do you say?

Are you kidding me?! You wake me up with your text messages for bowling??

I yawned so many times in a row and my mind was

too dull to keep count. All I wanted to do was lay in bed and just to go back sleep again. It was what I thought about as I slumped against the side of my bed, trying to close my eyes and go to sleep then and there. The sun shined directly in my face. I could also feel my body starting to get the energy to emerge fully out of the eight or nine-hour sleep that I placed it under. I knew it was too late to go back to sleep at that point. I had to rise and shine.

Shit! Thanks a lot, Derek!

I couldn't go back to sleep, so I retrieved my phone from off my bed and opened it. I went to my text message app and opened Derek's name. I replied to his text messages but not before I placed the volume on my phone way down so that the next time, I have a good night's sleep and it wouldn't be interrupted.

Ericka: Shouldn't we keep our focus on our secret mission of finding the shapeshifter and killing it?

I saw the three moving dots seconds later and got a new message from Derek.

Derek: We can't look for the shapeshifter until the night of a new moon, which won't be for another five days.

I saw the three dots again and a brand-new message from Derek.

Derek: I mean, shifters are somewhat active on most nights, regardless of the moon phase. They're not like werewolves. But the safe bet is to wait until a new moon in five days. That way, you and I know

for sure it'll be out hunting. And then, we'll hunt IT down.

Huh...interesting.

Ericka: Where did you get that info?

Derek: Josh.

Ericka: I shouldn't have even asked. I should've known.

Derek: Yeah. Monsters are the best resources for answers about other monsters. I guess you and I are lucky?

I managed to crack a small smile on my face. But it wasn't a laugh of entertainment. It was a laugh of ridicule. Every time Derek mentioned Josh's name, it was like my intuition was triggered. I couldn't help but find it laughable and ridiculous that Derek kept mentioning Josh. Because in my instincts, I know there was no 'Josh,' only a lying Derek. I just needed proof. Pronto.

I was interrupted from my thoughts about Josh when Derek sent me another message, which my phone alerted me to when it made a tiny vibrating buzz.

Derek: So, are we on for bowling tonight or not? Come on, it's not like we have anything to do while we wait for five days to come and go. It's alright, Ericka. We can focus on our mission of hunting down the shapeshifters and still live our lives. Plllee-asseee...go bowling with me. We were supposed to that weekend when...C'mon. I really want to hang out with you.

The desperation in Derek's messages was annoying. But he was right. I wasn't doing anything. I could use a change in atmosphere. I looked at the screen and saw the three moving dots again. Not long afterwards, Derek sent a new message.

Derek: It's not like it'll be a date or anything. It'll just be two friends hanging out with each other. Besides, you could use the fresh air. You need to get out of the house and change your atmosphere.

You read my mind...

I pondered all the points Derek made. But my brain was still feeling sleepy, although not as much as before. I decided that I needed a really big breakfast to have the energy and will to do anything, let alone bowling. If I were to go bowling with the guy who my instincts told me was the real wolf, I needed to fuel in the form of pancakes, eggs, bacon, and orange juice.

I shot Derek a text back.

Ericka: I'll let you know after breakfast.

I got a response from him a minute later.

Derek: Okay, fine. But don't keep me waiting for too long. I would really love to hang out with you.

Ericka: Yeah, I know. Me too. We'll talk later, 'kay?

Derek: Sure will. Bye for now.

Ericka: Byeeee.

I closed my phone and went to the bathroom to wash my face. I rummaged through my closet afterwards to wear something over my gray tank top, prior to taking off the complementary shorts. I found a pair of acid-washed skinny jeans along with a pair of black short-sleeve loose crop tees. I looked for my favorite green slip-on sneakers and I found them lying in a corner of the bedroom. I slipped into them and walked out of my room to the kitchen.

I could smell a wave of breakfast food through my nose as soon as I walked out of my room. The aroma of freshly scrambled eggs, pancakes, and bacon floated into my nostrils. It was the smell of Heaven. At least my morning was going to be bright when I ate my favorite breakfast.

I rushed into the kitchen as the smell of the breakfast got stronger in my nose. I saw MacKayla and her mother Victoria in the kitchen. Mrs. Devereaux had her back to the kitchen door and I looked at the back of her shoulder-length dark brown hair. MacKayla was on her phone sitting at the kitchen table. But when she saw me, she closed it and a bright wide smile was plastered over her face.

"Well, hello there, sleepy head! We were wondering when you would wake up. Have a seat," MacKayla said.

Her mother turned around and also had a big smile, too. I could see the laugh lines emerge around Mrs. Devereaux's light brown eyes and mouth as she looked at me with a kind motherly expression plastered on her face.

"Good morning, dear. I hope you slept well."

"Thank you, Mrs. Devereaux. I did."

Yeah, despite the loud ass phone I have thanks to Derek's text messages.

Mrs. Devereaux flashed that kind, motherly face at me one more time before turning back around and working on what looked like grilled cheese sandwiches. I looked at the table and saw a tray of the earlier things I smelled as I walked out of my room. MacKayla looked at me with that ridiculous smile she always has.

"These were getting kind of cold while you took that long-ass –"

MacKayla turned to look at her mom, not wanting to have a foul mouth near a lady with a strict no-tolerance rule for unruly language. She turned back to me and cracked a big smile again.

"That very long sleep. So, I heated them up in the microwave for you. Here, they're for you."

"Thanks. I appreciate it. My stomach is growling, so I need that."

I picked up a fork placed near the plate of eggs and started to eat them. MacKayla's mother turned around and held a plate of about seven grilled cheese sandwiches. She set them in the middle of the kitchen table in front of me and sat down from what I inferred was a long morning of cooking breakfast.

Mrs. Devereaux took a hair tie from her wrist and tied her hair up while MacKayla got off the phone and turned her attention to me. I was getting a big gulp of orange juice from a coffee mug.

"So, Ericka," Mrs. Devereaux said. "If you have nothing to do today, MacKayla and I are going to the mall. We're going to do some shopping and get our nails done. Would you like to join us?"

"Yeah, Ericka, come with us," MacKayla chimed in. "It'll be so fun with us three going. What do you say?"

It took me a second to remember Derek and him asking me out for bowling.

"That sounds amazing, Mrs. Devereaux. But I woke up this morning to a text message from my friend Derek asking me if I wanted to go bowling."

MacKayla and her mom shared a look of amusement between each other before turning their heads to me. I immediately knew what path they were taking.

"So, are you guys officially dating?" MacKayla asked.

"No, no, no. Don't get any funny ideas. We're just friends. I specifically told him we're just friends and that I'm not ready for a relationship with where I'm at in my life. This is nothing more than hanging out. It's not a date, by any means necessary."

MacKayla responded by forming an expression on her face that I could best describe in my mind as a "Really?" type of expression.

"I don't believe you," she then said.

"I'm serious. We're not dating!"

"MacKayla. Don't antagonize your friend."

"Thank you, Mrs. Devereaux. But you've given me a tough choice. Should I go with you guys or Derek? I mean, I might as well go with you so MacKayla here doesn't think I'm going on a date."

"Nonsense," Mrs. Devereaux said with a slight

frown on her face. "It sounds like this boy is trying to give you a good time. You should go with him. There'll be plenty more opportunities for us girls to hang out in the future. Besides, boys and girls can hang out without it being a date."

MacKayla parted her lips and rolled her eyes in response to what her mother directed at her.

"Are you sure?"

"Yes, Ericka," MacKayla then said. "Sorry for teasing you earlier. But it sounds like Derek is trying to make you happy. You need that. So, mom is right. We'll just do it another time. Go and have fun bowling and wipe the floor with him because you're a natural at it."

I chuckled at my friend's suggestion and nodded.

"Okay. I'll text him right now."

I got my phone out and shot a message to Derek.

Ericka: Hey, Derek. Looks like we're on for bowling. Can't wait to wipe the floor with you.

I immediately saw that Derek read my message and he was already typing up his reply. My phone made a small buzz and I saw his new message.

Derek: Yes! You are so on! I can't wait. How does 7 sound?

Ericka: Sounds good. See you then.

I put my phone away and finished eating breakfast. If I was going to beat another pro in a game like mine, I needed to fuel up and get my energy and game on. Grilled cheese was a bonus energy boost for my stomach, too, which I made sure to wolf down after I ate everything on the tray.

Derek and I went to a bowling alley not far from where I lived called the Spares-N-Strikes Center. Once Derek and I stepped foot inside the place, I saw families, friends, and couples playing while others were getting ready to play and putting their shoes on. The smell of chili cheese fries, French fries, chicken tenders, and hotdogs curled inside my nose, which activated my taste buds to unleash a lake of mouth water.

I took my mind off the food, though, seeing it as a distraction. I had to be on top of my game and focused on beating Derek. I didn't want to underestimate my opponent, not knowing how good or bad he was. I just had to see for myself.

"So, what do you say we play just one game?" Derek asked.

"Whatever floats your boat. Just know that I'm going to wipe these lanes with you when I'm done."

Derek gave out a hearty laugh from his diaphragm and turned back to me.

"We'll see about that."

We went to a lane in the middle of the ten lanes inside the bowling center. I saw Derek put on some monster grip bowling gloves and they looked like the same ones I had. Derek looked at me in amazement when he saw me put my gloves on.

"So, it appears that we're alike in so many ways," he quipped.

"I guess we are."

Derek made a small chuckle and went first. He grabbed a large, orange bowling ball and rolled it towards the pins. He hit all the pins and got a strike, seeing how good he was. He turned back to me with the biggest smile on his face and pumped his fist, while I shook my head at his early and premature boast.

"You're turn, my lady," he said as he walked up to me.

"I'll turn that smile upside down."

I walked up to the bowling ball rack and grabbed a medium-sized blue ball. I rolled the ball towards the pins and managed to strike only six pins. I could imagine in my head that Derek was cheesing like a little kid at the early advantage he had, but at least I managed to get a spare in the next frame.

The smile on Derek's face when I turned around was pretty much as I imagined it. The corners of his lips almost reached up to his ears as I shook my head when my eyes met his.

"It's the beginning of the game. I'm always rusty in the beginning of the game. Give me time and I'll beat you."

"Yeah, yeah. Excuses."

I playfully pushed Derek on his right arm as he went to take his turn. The game was dominated by both of us seeing how many strikes we could get, and which one would get the most strikes. The end result was me having more strikes than Derek and I won the game by a score of 220 to 200.

Derek looked at me with a flabbergasted expression on his face and enjoyed the reaction all the way to our cars.

"Oh my gosh…you really are a pro! How could I have underestimated you?"

"Don't know. But if it makes you feel better, you are by far the best opponent I've ever faced in bowling. No one has ever gotten past 150 with me, let alone 200."

Derek nodded and I could tell he was amazed by my skills. The expression of surprise faded away from his dimpled cheeks and he reached his hand out to me.

"Good game?"

"Good game," I said as I reached my hand out to him.

"But no, seriously, Ericka. Thanks for letting me hang out with you. It was really fun. To be honest, it wasn't really about the competition or beating you and you beating me. It was more about spending time with you. So, thanks for letting me see you and hang out with you. It means a lot to me. You have no idea how much you made my night, and how happy you made me tonight."

I could feel my cheeks blushing and growing rosy by what Derek said. My insides also felt warm and fuzzy.

"You are so sweet. It was my pleasure. We'll do it again sometime soon. Thanks to you too, I guess. I had a good time."

"I'm glad, and yes, we will absolutely do this again soon."

Derek and I stood at our cars, silent and looking around the parking lot with nothing to talk about. The atmosphere between us was so thick it could be sliced like a piece of pie. I could smell small whiffs of his cologne as I didn't hear much noise from the public outside. It was like time froze just for us, so we can talk and interact more, so that we couldn't waste any more minutes standing in awkward silence.

"So…" Derek said. "Have your parents ever taken you bowling when you were younger?"

"A couple of times, but not as often."

"Really? So how did you get good at it?"

"I would come here by myself and play. Just to relieve stress from school and life around me. I would also practice on my best friends and I would beat them."

"I see. You were really good; I shouldn't have under-estimated you."

"Thanks for realizing that."

Derek nodded and smiled at me before we went back to more of the same quiet time earlier.

"Maybe I should get going," he said. "It was such a good night hanging out with you, Ericka. I'll talk to you soon."

Derek started to walk away from me when I realized I didn't want our night to end on a pathetic, uncomfortable series of moments between us.

"Wait!"

He stopped walking away from me and turned around to look at me.

"What is it?"

"There's something I want to say."

Derek took a few steps forward towards me and had a curious look on his face.

"You have no idea how much I appreciate you being in my life at this point in it. After losing my mom and my aunt, I feel like I'm not lonely because of you. I have someone to turn to for comfort and for a shoulder to lean on. I can't express to you enough how much you mean to me. You are so sweet and kind."

Derek gave a shy grin from his refined cheeks.

"Thanks. You're sweet and kind, too. And I'm glad I can be here for you in your time of need."

"Mhm. And I just want to say I'm so sorry for all the times I've been suspicious of you being the werewolf. You've trained me and taught me how to use weapons when I didn't know who else would. I don't know how to make it up to you to do that. All I can say is that I'm truly sorry for accusing you of being the wolf and that I'll make it up to you for all the wonderful training sessions."

"You don't need to, it's not necessary. I was just helping you so you can fight the shapeshifter."

I walked closer to Derek and took his big hands in mine.

"I want to, Derek. For you. And I feel like saying thank you and showing appreciation isn't enough. So, I want to do something for you one day."

I pulled Derek gently towards me. I wrapped both of my arms around his large back and could feel all the muscles contained beneath his massive skin. He wrapped one arm around my hair and the other around my back. It was like being a baby, comforted in the warmth of a blanket woven in the fabric of love. I liked Derek's size because I always felt my small body snug and restful in his arms. He knew how to make me feel bliss in my life every time his fingers touched my skin.

11

Five days came and went while I sat on eggshells waiting anxiously for the night of a new moon to arrive. I could see glimpses of it through the thick trees of the forest when I was alone, while the smell of the damp, wet earth and the rotten, decayed wood feasted on by the decomposers of the forest welcomed me when it entered my nose.

I could hear various things in the forest that made my nerves tingle. Small twigs breaking on the ground, the leaves and branches of trees shaking and rustling from the small wind of the night, and the calls of nocturnal birds in the forest all made their way into my ear. I even saw a couple of barred owls gawking at me with their small but soulless, colorless beady eyes. It was as if they were expecting something to happen to me.

I was alone in the forest freaking out about every small thing because Derek wasn't here with me. He told me he would meet up with me in the forest so we could hunt and kill the shapeshifter but so far, he's been a no-show. Meanwhile, I was over here stewing with anger at him for leaving me alone is this God-forsaken forest, vulnerable to an ambush by the shapeshifter at any time.

I would think he wasn't standing me up, that instead he was hatching some type of plan to catch the shapeshifter off guard and lure it to us so we can kill it tonight. But he should've at least had the decency to tell me first instead of going rogue and doing something on his own. Anyways, I wasn't completely weak and vulnerable.

I was equipped with daddy's machete and I gripped it very tight in my hand. I gripped it so tight I could feel my own sweat on the handle. I was nervous as hell. That shapeshifter could come out any second and finish me off. I was so nervous that I scared the fuck out of myself when I stepped on a small tree branch and snapped it in half. I thought something was near me. I thought *it* was near me.

If I wasn't scared enough by the tree branch snapping, I was sure as hell frightened to death when I heard a large and loud male scream in the forest. My heart started beating at an abnormally fast pace. The scream continued and the more I listened to it, the more I started to panic. It was in the distance and no other male would be in the forest except for...

"Derek!"

No answer. He was in trouble and I had to run to

him as fast as I could. I heard the scream again and ran in its direction. I determined it was to the north of where I stood in the forest. I ran in the direction of the scream, with every second and nanosecond hoping to the heavens that Derek wasn't hurt.

"Derek! I'm coming!"

"Ericka! Help me!"

Oh, fuck!

"I'm coming!"

He was really in danger. I hoped and prayed to God that he wasn't hurt as I ran to the sound of his screaming. He let out another scream and, in that moment, I knew I was getting close. I came to a clearing and stood my ground. I waited for Derek to let me know where he was. I wanted him to scream another time so I could determine where he was. The screaming ceased, though. The forest went back to the same silence I heard when I came here.

I was starting to feel emotional, and I felt tears trying to form. My heart was also heavy as I tried to catch my breath. I felt the sweat wetting my hair after all the running I did. I couldn't hear him anymore. What if the shapeshifter killed Derek? What if he's dead?

"Derek!"

I screamed his voice multiple times, just waiting for a response. I wanted to hear his voice again so bad. I would've done anything to hear Derek's voice again. I fell to my knees and started crying. I might have just heard my best friend's last words. He was helpless as I tried to get to him, but I couldn't save him. Derek was probably defenseless, without a weapon, as the shapeshifter tore his heart out and ate it in front of his bloody carcass.

"Ericka?"

I heard his voice. I ceased crying the second I heard his voice. I gasped when I heard Derek call my name. I turned around and looked at his face. It was him alright. The same guy who I met in the cafeteria with spiky brown hair and bright green eyes that fascinated me the first time I saw them.

"Derek? Is that really you?"

I wiped the tears rolling down my cheeks as I walked up towards him. I saw a worried look on his face. He tried to understand what was wrong with me and why I was crying. It was as if I didn't hear him screaming for help like ten minutes ago. I looked at him and saw he was completely alright. No blood, no chest cavity. He was intact and still breathing.

"Is everything alright?"

I stood about fifteen feet from him with rage and hatred boiling in my eyes. I couldn't see any of the colors of the forest. Instead, I saw nothing but red.

"No, everything is not fucking alright! I thought you were in fucking danger! You screamed my name and you called for help! I thought you were fucking dead, you asshole! I thought the shapeshifter got to you and ripped your heart out!"

"I'm sorry but I'm fine. Look at me, I'm alive and fine."

"Yeah, I can see that you moron! Why the fuck did you scare me like that? I ran through this fucking forest looking for you and I fell to my fucking knees when I thought you were dead!"

"I'm so sorry, Ericka. Please."

He started to walk towards me and reached his arms out like he was about to hug me. I started to walk backwards because I wasn't in any mood for that shit.

"We need to find the shapeshifter. Once we find it and kill it, I hope, then we'll discuss this prank of yours and I'll decide if I rip your head off or spare your life."

Derek put his arms down at that moment and formed a wide smile on his face. It wasn't a normal smile. I sensed that it was an evil smile of a malicious nature, like he waited to do something to me.

"What's so fucking funny?" I asked Derek with a furious tone rolling off my tongue.

"We don't need to find the shapeshifter."

I squinted my eyes at Derek, feeling very confused.

"What? What the hell are you talking about?"

"I'm right here, darling."

Derek peeled his lips back and revealed two rows of prickly teeth on the top and bottom. All the anger left my body and was replaced with horror and shock. I was lured to this clearing by the shapeshifter. It was all just a ploy. The shifter transformed to my appearance and ejected the claws out of its fingers.

"Ready to have fun?" it said, with my voice.

"Fuck you!"

The shifter's smile was gone. It now had a look of

anger on its face. I was ready with my machete for its imminent attack.

"I know what you are. I'm aware of monsters in this world. Your race is one of them. Why did you kill my aunt?"

The monster looked at my weapon and the look on its face was serious. It knew that it couldn't mess with me or underestimate me anymore. It knew that it couldn't fuck with me anymore. The shifter shrugged as a start to my response.

"I was just in the area and was hungry. Your aunt and her guest had these delicious, juicy hearts that I wanted to feast on so bad."

My blood steamed and raged as I fumed from the monster's taunts.

"Your aunt was so helpless. She didn't know what she was looking at, or *who* she was looking at for that matter. When she saw herself in me, you should've seen the look on her face. It was priceless. But it wasn't as gratifying as the look of terror on her face when I sunk my claws into her and ripped her heart out!"

"Shut the fuck up!"

The shapeshifter reverted back to its cynical smile and chuckled.

"I'm going to fucking kill you for what you did to her. I'm going to avenge Aunt Carrie's death. One way or the other, you will die. Tonight."

"How, on earth, will you do that? If you have this knowledge about monsters, you know by now that there's only one source of information on how to kill all monsters and no one can find it. Not even us, let alone any humans. And since you have knowledge about my race, let's do a little quiz, shall we? Is it true that despite having human appearances, we have a true form of our own?"

I looked at the shapeshifter confused and surprised as hell. I didn't have the guts in me to answer its question because I was scared at the fact that it had its race had its own true form. The shapeshifter shook its head at me and gave me a pathetic smile.

"The answer is...we do have our own form. A little description for you: thin, insect-like dark brown body with long, thin fingers and legs with claws on each. Just a little taste of our look. So how are you going to end my life tonight, little missy? You don't even know what we truly look like."

I looked at the shapeshifter with hatred and all the ire in the world.

"You'll see. Because I don't give two rats' asses about what you look like. I just want you dead."

I raised my blade and waved it in the shapeshifter's face. The monster didn't waver. It only smiled even more and gave out a small laugh.

"Well, come on then. Give me your best shot."

The monster taunted me by raising one of its claws towards me and wagging it at me, telling me to charge at it. The smile on its face lit the fuse of the bomb that was inside me. I exploded and charged at it with my machete.

"*Mittent*" I heard the shapeshifter say as it waved its

hands and threw me through the air several feet away from it and onto the ground. The impact of landing on the dirt was so hard I lost grip of my machete. I roiled on the ground as I saw the shapeshifter come towards me. My blade was within reach. I reached for it and grabbed it, waiting to strike against the shapeshifter once it came near me.

The shapeshifter came near me and blurted another phrase, while springing forth its right hand – *rigescunt indutae*. All of a sudden, my entire body froze. I couldn't move on the ground. I was immobile and couldn't lift a single muscle or part of my body. The shapeshifter bent to the ground and stroked my hair. I was scared beyond any type of measure. I was about to die, frozen in place and thinking that the shapeshifter will end my life then and there.

"You are one tough girl, Ericka Jones. You have the courage to come into my forest and try to kill me with a puny blade. But at least you showed guts. And now, you'll die a painful, slow death. Tell your aunt I said hi."

I wanted to feel anger at the monster for its gibe. I wanted to get up and just try to kill it. But I wasn't able to. This phrase that the shifter screamed at me, whether it was Latin, Italian, or whatever, did me in. The shifter flashed its prickled teeth at me and raised its claws, ready to sink them into my heart.

Then, the shifter looked up in awe when it and I heard a very familiar sound – the howling of a wolf.

"Fuck!" I heard it say.

A combined feeling of relief and surprise overcame

me. The shapeshifter had a look on its face as it looked all around for the werewolf. It was then that the wolf came out of the forest and charged at the shapeshifter, ready for a fight. The werewolf pounced on the shifter and tackled it to the ground away from me.

The freeze the shapeshifter put on me was lifted from my body and I was able to move again. My entire body shook as I got off the dirt of the forest and was able to move again. I looked at my machete and picked it up immediately, ready to help the wolf with the shapeshifter. I saw the werewolf on top of the shifter biting it in its neck like that night I first saw it.

The monster screamed the same inhumane scream I heard that night. It was in agony as it slashed at the wolf's sides with its own claws. I could tell the wolf, Josh, was in agony as I heard it make small whimpering sounds while its fangs were sunk in the monster's neck. But Josh wouldn't budge and instead just pinned his canine teeth into the monster's neck.

I looked at the fur on Josh's side and saw blood streaming out, a sight that scared me to death.

"Josh!"

The werewolf finally retracted its claws from the shifter's neck, and it turned its attention to me. The accidental distraction gave the shifter the opportunity to take advantage over the wolf by throwing it off and pouncing on it while it was on the ground. The shifter dug its claws into the wolf's sides, and I heard the wolf howl in pain. At the same time, the wounds on the shifter's neck began to self-heal, a sight that frightened me to death.

I took it as my cue to charge at the shifter to get it off the wolf. I slashed at the shifter's arms and kept slashing at them in blind anger. I wasn't even thinking about what I was doing. I only thought about the words "Slash, girl, slash!" as I kept cutting at the shapeshifter's skin. It was at that point I saw steam rising from the shapeshifter's skin where I gashed it.

Its screaming filled my ears to the point where I was almost deaf. But I know that with each inhumane yelp from the shifter, I gained the satisfaction of causing it pain. It didn't last long though as the shifter yelled the word *"Mittent!"* and sent me through the air to the ground several feet away from it. I looked up and saw the shapeshifter flee into the dense forest at a super-human speed.

My mind raced to the werewolf as I got up from the ground. Josh was hurt and I had to check on him. Once I got on my feet, I saw nothing in sight. Josh was nowhere to be found. I looked for him immediately. A brief search ended when I heard a male scream in the distance.

"Josh!"

I ran towards the scream as fast as I could. Even though I was mostly out of breath from the run I had earlier and from all the ghastly physical activities that followed, I still ran as fast as I could to follow the sound of Josh's screaming. I got closer to the bawling and walked carefully towards it. I found the source of the screaming, but it wasn't Josh.

I found Derek on the ground, slumped against a tree and naked from head to toe. His sides near where his kidneys are were seeping blood. I also saw his fangs start to retract and the wounds on his side from the shapeshifter's attack begin to self-heal on their own. Once they self-healed fully, Derek's canine fangs were completely retracted. All that was left was blood where the wounds on his sides were.

It was all the evidence I needed to confirm my instincts as I looked at Derek in horror with tears rolling down my eyes. He turned his attention to me, and I saw he had the same look of horror on his face when he looked into my eyes once I found out his secret.

"Ericka," he said as he started to get emotional. "Please –"

"I fucking knew it! All along, you've been lying to me! There is no fucking 'childhood friend' named Josh! It was you the entire time and you lied to my fucking face, you bastard!"

"I can explain, please –"

"Get the hell away from me! I don't want to see you ever again for as long as I live! You lied to me and you hurt me in the deepest way possible. You lied to me! I can't believe I trusted you all this time and showed admiration and appreciation towards you!"

"I'm so sorry! Please, if you just wait –"

"I'm done with you! You stay away from me! Forget

that you even know me! Erase me from your mind and from your life! Lose my number and don't contact me ever again! I don't want anything to do with you anymore! You're a werewolf and I want you to stay away from me!"

I dashed away from Derek as fast as I could. I turned around for a split second and I saw him on his knees crying. I had no sympathy for him. All I thought about at that point was just leaving the forest and never seeing his face for as long as I lived.

12

W ell, it happened. My worst fear came true. Ericka now hates my guts and is afraid of me. The cat was out of the bag despite all my attempts to stuff it in there as best as possible. I switched back to wolf form and ran to my cabin as fast as I could. I felt so many tears well up in my eyes that I couldn't see properly where I was going. I kept blinking and closing my eyelids to push the tears out, but it didn't help much.

I ran past the two wolves who were placed on the lookout by my uncle. I just wanted to go inside the cabin and cry my eyes out until tomorrow. I transformed back into human form and I twisted the doorknob so fast before I burst into my cabin and ran into the living room. I laid face down on one of the couches and soaked the fabric of the pillow with my tears. I absorbed the warmth of the couch up against my body and I took comfort in it.

I haven't let myself be vulnerable to anyone in my life, and I certainly haven't been this close to anyone either. Ever since my dad died at the hands of my uncle, my heart has turned to stone. That was until I gave Ericka the keys to access it. Then not only did the stones melt away, but it grew four sizes. My heart grew for her. She became my weak spot.

I've been running away for so long that I'm actually a stray. Stray wolves are a big no-no in the werewolf race. We either belong in packs or we spend the rest of our lives defending ourselves from pack alphas who want to make us a part of them. I don't want to join a pack more than I don't want to give up meat.

I want to be a free wolf for the rest of my life because there's nothing oppressive more than living under the rule of a pureblood alpha. I value my freedom more than any pack on this earth and I haven't been part of a pack ever since my dad's untimely and violent passing. I wanted to make sure it stayed that way.

That's why my uncle is in Appleton with his wolf pack. I can't fight against a pack on my own, so I got my uncle to come here from Washington. He wanted a chance to make it up to me and I needed someone to help me fight off any pack that may force me to join. It was a win-win situation, even though the idea made me sick to my stomach. But I'm desperate. I need all the aid I can get.

I spent so much time on the couch crying over Ericka that I lost track of time. I felt like I've been crying for ten minutes, maybe even twenty. Who knows? Time was now frozen in my life. It felt like my life stopped because Ericka was no longer in it. Everything stopped because Ericka was gone. I knew instantly she didn't want to be associated with a werewolf. She thinks I might kill her or something, even though I wouldn't lay a hand on her other than to give her a hug or for a sweet intimate moment.

How was I going to convince her of that now? She's probably thinking about so many ways to block me out of her life and cut off all contact with me. What's even worse is that she might go to the authorities and alert them to a werewolf in Appleton's forest, and they'll hunt me down along with the other wolves here. I would have to put up a fight and they would, too. It would be a fucking massacre with bodies and blood everywhere. It would gather national attention and the media would be all over it.

I didn't give any more thought to these theories. It was all speculation, and I didn't want to go that far. Maybe Ericka wasn't like that. Maybe she would just want to forget all about me and bury the memories about me so far deep she wouldn't even speak my name to anyone ever again. But that's not what I wanted. I have to win her back. I can't let her slip out of my life. I can't lose her. I feel a strong connection to her.

But I couldn't think about how to get Ericka back in my life. I couldn't even cry anymore. I was startled off the couch when I heard growling and howling outside my cabin. I wiped all the tears on my face and ran outside the door. I saw a wolf I haven't seen before ambushed and killed the two lookouts.

The wolf was sinking his teeth deep into the heart of one of the wolves when I ran out. He had brownish-red fur. He raised his head and hackles up, and looked at me with a rage in his eyes. The wolf growled at me and showed me his fangs. I squinted my eyes and turned into my wolf form within a matter of seconds.

Even though I just came back from a fight with the shapeshifter, I was fueled by so much anger and hatred towards being exposed to Ericka for who I was. I saved her from it so she should be thankful for saving her a second time. Maybe she'll forgive me with time, and I took solace in that. But it was a second-long solace as I charged at the wolf for a fight.

He charged at me and pounced on me, but I jumped underneath the wolf and tackled him to the ground with my claws. I later saw myself on top of the wolf after hearing the loud thud of impact when he hit the ground. I was on top of him with my claws deep into his guts, slashing at him with a furious sequence of movements. I even sunk them deep into the wolf where I felt some of his insides.

I heard the wolf wail and howl from all the pain, but I couldn't feel anything but anger and fury. I was blind with those feelings. I didn't care if the wolf cried or screamed from all the pain I was causing him. All I felt was this pure wrath and all I tasted was the wolf's throat as I ripped the skin apart, and my fangs sinking deeper into his voice box.

It was then that he stopped howling and I heard something else instead. I heard bones breaking, like something detaching from something else. After the fight was over, I didn't feel anymore anger. I could see in front of me again and I was able to see every other color than red. I looked down at the wolf underneath my paws and saw a pool of blood around his dead, *decapitated* body.

Those are the bones that I heard break. I killed him in such a frenzy that I cringed when I looked down at his corpse and saw the claw marks and cavities I created in his stomach. I backed away from the wolf and turned back into human. I walked back to the cabin and just left the wolf's body to rot.

I didn't go inside. I stayed for a few minutes on the porch and sat down in a chair. All I thought about now was the future as I looked up at the moon. I hoped that Ericka would move on from tonight. I hoped that she would forgive me for lying to her like that. We're meant to be together. She can't forget about my kindness to her and the times I saved her from the shapeshifter.

She has to forgive me eventually. She will. I will work hard to ensure she does if it's the last thing I do on this earth.

13

I didn't want to wake up. I didn't feel like opening my eyes and facing the world that I lived in. I could feel the sun radiating outside through my bedroom window. My eyes, though, weren't ready to open. I struggled to lift my eyelids and wake up. I just wanted to sleep and stay asleep for as long as possible.

All of my slumber eventually left me, and I was able to wake up. I lifted my head off the pillow with squinting eyes after looking at the bright sun. It was then that I gathered the energy and will to get up from my bed and leave my bedroom. I went to the bathroom directly across the hall and splashed water on my crusty face. I brushed the untamed wavy blonde hair I had and returned it to its normal form.

Once I did all my business in the bathroom, I walked back into my bedroom and shut the door. I didn't feel like leaving my bedroom other than to go to the bathroom if it became necessary. My stomach had too many knots for me to eat or drink anything. I didn't feel like doing anything except to cover myself all snug and warm underneath the blanket of my bed and stare at the ceiling. All I knew was that my life was going nowhere, and I didn't even want to attempt to ponder where it would go or might go at some point in the future. Whatever happens next happens.

I hopped back onto bed and covered myself in my blanket. I stared up at the ceiling and looked at the white space. It was a perfect analogy of my current life right now – just a white space with nothing in it. Nothing has happened in my life nor will anything happen that'll make it a good life.

I knew all along that Derek lied to me, but he hid his secret to me in such an intricate way. Even though I believed in my gut that Derek was the werewolf the entire time, I was still naïve and stupid to believe that the wolf I saw last night was his nonexistent childhood friend. I screamed out the name Josh when I saw Derek being hurt because of what he put in my head.

I shouldn't have even entertained the idea in my mind. I should've just built a brain guard in my mind or a tin foil hat to put on my head to block out stupid stories, lies, and half-ass excuses from who I thought was my best friend. I've never been this stupid in my life. I can't believe I let someone like Derek Bentley take advantage of me and take me for a fool. It won't happen again.

But my mind was conflicted with how good of a guy he was. He was so sweet to me the first time I met him. He helped me train in weapon use and even saved me all those times from the shapeshifter. And yet he betrayed me. How could such a sweet guy like Derek deceive me and do something like that to me? Was that all an act? I couldn't just forget all the good things he did for me. Did he lie to me because he was afraid of my reaction to him being a wolf? Was I being too rough on him?

I wanted to delve deeper into this, but my train of thought was interrupted by something else while I stared at the ceiling. The thought of the mission to avenge my aunt came to mind. Where do I go now? What do I do now to get justice for my aunt's death? I was going to work with Derek on killing the shapeshifter using his expertise in the supernatural, since I thought he was friends with a monster.

How was I going to find and kill the shapeshifter now? How do I kill it without Derek? I felt more lost than a kid at a Fall festival maze. What complicated things even more was the mission to find Bart Ramsay's book. How the hell do I even do that now with Derek no longer in my life?

You just have to wing it, girl. Just stab and slash that shapeshifter everywhere in its body. The heart should be right in its chest, right? It has to be!

Without the help of a werewolf or anyone with knowledge about the world of the supernatural, I was just going to have to wing it. Either I find a witch to help me locate the book or I wing it by finding that shifter and sinking my machete into every fiber and skin of its frame. I couldn't help but be overcome by my emotions.

I started crying once all of these thoughts ran in my mind. I sat up in my bed and placed my face into the palms of both my hands. I cried because Derek committed a serious offense against me, and I let him do it. I let myself be deceived by him when I should've just trusted my guts. I needed evidence that he was lying about being a werewolf and I got what I wanted.

My eyes feasted last night on the sight of Derek, naked in the forest with his fangs still jutting out inside his mouth while his wounds started to self-heal. Those flash images ran across my mind as I cried heavily. The images represented the lies Derek told me and were a constant reminder of how much he took advantage of me.

But then again, the thoughts of how sweet and kind he was to me came back. He saved me from the shifter; he trained me to shoot guns, arrows, and taught me self-defense; and he nursed me back to health at his cabin. I forgot all about that. This guy lied through his teeth and hurt me in such a bad, disgusting way. Yet he did so much for me at the same time.

Fuck, what was I supposed to do??

It was then that I heard a knock on the door.

"Ericka? You awake?" MacKayla asked. "I thought I heard you go into the bathroom. If you're still asleep, sorry hun. I'll make it up to you today."

I wiped the majority of my tears off as hard as I could. I used my shirt, my blanket, anything I could use in my room to wipe those tears away. I gathered myself and looked like I had just woken up, even roughing up my hair a little bit.

"No, it's alright. Come in."

MacKayla cheerfully opened my bedroom door and had a big smile on her face when she walked into my bedroom. But the smile on her face was extinguished in favor of a more serious look.

"Oh my gosh, I'm so sorry for waking you up. I'll make it up to you, Ericka. I promise! There's this arcade that just opened up near downtown, so I'll take you to it. It'll be my treat."

"I don't know. I have to apply for jobs today and I feel bad that you would have to pay for both of us. Can we go another time?"

MacKayla's face shifted from serious to downright concerned. I was scared she might have figured from my groggy and weakened voice that I cried. She also grabbed my cheeks and studied my eyes to see if anything was wrong with me.

"Why are your eyes red, Ericka? And why do you sound like you've just been crying?"

"I don't know what you're talking about."

"Bullshit. I know when you're lying to me. I can sense when something is up with you. I'm one of your best friends, remember? The reason why you don't want me to take you to the arcade has nothing to do with jobs or feeling bad about me paying. So, tell me what's going on."

"You're being dramatic."

"I'm not leaving this room until you tell me what's going on."

MacKayla crossed her arms and widened her deep brown eyes. All the tears that I tried so hard to conceal from my best friend came back. I grabbed my blanket and buried my face in it so MacKayla wouldn't see me.

"Oh my gosh! I knew it! Ericka!"

I could feel MacKayla hugging me in her arms as I let go of my blanket. She held me up to her left shoulder as she lowered her head towards the top of mine. I could feel her soft face on my scalp as she comforted me and rubbed my arms with her right hand.

"Honey, why are you crying? What's wrong? I knew something was wrong!"

"I'm just feeling so bad and miserable right now."

"You should've talked to me about it. Come on, spill it, Ericka. Don't make me beg you to tell me what's going on."

I had to lie to her. I didn't want anyone I knew to know about monsters. More importantly, I didn't want my sister-figure best friend to know that Derek was a werewolf who broke my heart into a million pieces by lying to me and making me look stupid. I couldn't tell MacKayla he was a werewolf to begin with. I had to come up with a lie on the spot.

I let go of MacKayla's arms, which forced her to let go of me. I wiped a few tears away as I tried to maintain my composure long enough so I could talk to her.

"It happened six days ago when I went bowling with Derek. Let's just say, we're not friends anymore."

"Oh my gosh. Did he do or say anything to you?"

"No, he didn't do anything. He didn't hurt me physically, as you can tell."

"Good, because I'll break his neck if he does. What happened, honey? Tell me what Derek did."

"It's not what he did. It's what he said."

I looked at MacKayla and gaged the suspense in her face. She was waiting so bad for me to reveal what Derek said. She wanted to find him and try to beat the living daylight out of him. But I didn't want her anywhere near him. He's a werewolf and might transform and kill MacKayla in self-defense if he's threatened.

This dark thought and many others occupied a corner of my brain. She might see him somewhere in public and do something crazy to embarrass him in front of everyone, which would cause her to look like a pariah and Derek look like a punk. Either way, it wasn't a good outcome if these two met after today.

"OMG, Ericka! Just fucking tell me what this douchebag said!"

"You have to promise me not to do anything stupid against him if I tell you. I know how you are. I need you to promise me you won't confront him, accost him, or even approach Derek to talk to him. Please. I don't want you to get in trouble or anything. Promise me or I won't say a word."

"Ugh, okay!"

MacKayla sarcastically placed a hand on her chest and raised the other hand in the air.

"I solemnly swear not to do anything stupid to land me in trouble."

"I'm serious, MacKayla!"

"Okay! I promise you I won't do anything stupid to Derek or even interact with him! Happy? Now please, tell me what's going on!"

I wiped whatever tears were left on my cheeks before I turned to MacKayla and told her a fabricated story about Derek.

"It all happened six days ago when I went bowling with Derek. Him and I had just completed a game of bowling and I won. But he was angry at me because I won, and he accused me of cheating. I told him there was no way I cheated because he saw me play fair the entire time."

"How did he say you were cheating?"

"He said I used a ball lighter than his and that my game gloves gave me such an advantage over him. I was like, 'What the hell? You wore gloves, too!' and yeah, I did use a lighter ball because I'm smaller than him. If I used the same size ball he used, it would've given him the advantage and I would've felt like he was cheating."

MacKayla shook her head, and I could see her face getting red. I could tell she started to get angry and was contemplating breaking the promise she made me earlier not to confront Derek.

"MacKayla?"

"I'm listening. Just go on."

"You promised me not to do anything. Don't get in trouble because of this jerk. He's not worth it."

"I know, Ericka. I'm listening, just continue."

MacKayla grabbed my hands and placed them into hers. She cracked a small smile at me to reassure me everything was alright, which gave me the confidence to keep telling her my story…or my lie.

"Anyways, I told him that it was just a game and not to take it too seriously. He said that if it was just a game then I shouldn't have cheated. I raised my voice at him and cursed at him. I told him I didn't cheat and that I won fair and square. He yelled back at me and cursed at me."

"Oh my gosh, honey, I'm so sorry."

I could feel MacKayla's hands gripping mine tight. It was like she squeezed my hands to release her anger, treating my fingers as some kind of stress balls. I let go of her hands and she immediately realized the error of her actions.

"I'm sorry. I'm just so angry at this prick right now."

"I know but you made me a promise. Besides, I didn't get to the worst part."

"Oh my gosh, there's a worst part?"

"Yes. The argument ended when he told me that my parents would be proud of raising a cheater."

MacKayla gasped and covered her gaping mouth. I nodded in response to her reaction. I felt awful bringing my deceased parents into my lie. But I had to make the story convincing to my best friend. MacKayla knew bullshit when she smelled it. She was the type of person whose eyes were invulnerable from wool being pulled over them. That's why I was surprised when she believed me.

"Are you serious?" she asked.

"Mhm."

"Oh my gosh, that mother-"

"Hey! Don't even."

"He disrespected your dead parents! How can I not?"

"I told him we were no longer friends and that I never wanted to see his face again."

"If I were you, I would knee that son of a bitch right in his man parts! Oh my gosh, Ericka! I'm really sorry he disrespected you and your parents like that."

"You don't have to apologize for something that assclown said."

MacKayla nodded and we hugged briefly before she let me go and a look of confusion formed on her face.

"What?" I asked.

"Why didn't you tell me this earlier? This happened six days ago. You held onto this incident for six days, bottled up inside you without telling me about it?"

I knew I couldn't get anything past MacKayla. She was like a detective who left nothing unturned. Hell, I wouldn't be surprised if she worked in law enforcement one day. But since I created the whole story about the argument between Derek and I out of the air with ease, I had no problem creating one more lie now.

"I don't know, I just wanted to keep my problems to myself and not bother you or your family with my issues. Besides, I was successful at it until last night when I saw Derek at the movies with another friend. I just ran out of the theater and to my car as fast as I could."

I told MacKayla and her mom that I was going to the movies by myself as a ploy to go to the forest and confront the shapeshifter. They told me to have a good time. MacKayla shook her head in disappointment.

"I can't believe you would keep something like this from me. We're practically sisters. You're not a burden when you tell me your problems. And as far as my family's concerned, they're as cool as me. We adopted you because we love you and care about you. You shouldn't have tortured yourself by keeping this inside you for almost a week."

"I know. I'm sorry, okay? Next time I'll be more honest. How's that?"

"Thank you. You should. Come here."

MacKayla took me in her arms, and she held me in the warmest way a sister would. She stroked my hair and comforted me, while I kept feeling horrible for lying to her and kept thinking about how much of a scumbag Derek was. I gripped MacKayla's arms as she stopped rubbing the strands of my hair.

"Tell you what. You don't need that sorry excuse of a human being in your life. And you certainly don't need to cry because of him. He's not worth it. I'm glad you're done with him. I have a great idea of what we can do to get you out of this misery."

MacKayla and I ended our hug and I looked at her

with my crusty eyes. She wiped any remaining tears underneath my eyes.

"What's that?"

"I'm taking you to the arcade I mentioned earlier."

"Oh my gosh, MacKayla. I already told you I have to look for jobs today. I meant it when I said it."

"I'm taking you no matter what. No ifs, ands, or buts about it."

"You're going to make me do something I don't want to do?"

"Yes, because I love you and I don't want you wallowing in this funk anymore. I'm taking you to the arcade and that's it."

I managed to crack a smile on my face and MacKayla had one, too. She grabbed me into her arms again and I felt peace and bliss when MacKayla held me.

14

Yesterday was a fun day with MacKayla after she convinced me to go to this new arcade with her. We played games like *Dance Revolution, Pac-Man, Donkey Kong, Galaga, Centipede, Street Fighter,* and *Space Invaders.* I forgot the other games that we played but we had the most fun in a long time. I forgot all my worries and problems with MacKayla and Derek were nonexistent in my mind.

But it was a time to be serious today. One of the jobs that I applied for called me back requesting an interview. It was for an FOH position at a local eatery called Riley Jr.'s. It took me a brief period of time to figure out what that stood for before I searched it up on Google and saw 'Front of House.'

I walked into the restaurant and saw it was lively. Nearly every table and booth was filled with folks of all ages, eating their lunch. The restaurant was about 15-17 square feet in size and could seat about thirty guests at once. I could smell what I thought was a potato odor, the smell of fresh grilled steak, and hand-tossed lettuce.

"Hi. Welcome to Riley, Jr.'s! How may I help you?"

I saw a woman standing behind a terminal at the front counter. She was a few feet taller than me with her blonde hair in a ponytail and wearing the company's cap. I saw her name imprinted on a tag that was hooked to the cap – Suzanne. Suzanne looked to be in her mid or late thirties.

"Hi, I'm here for an interview."

"Wonderful! You can sit anywhere you want, and the manager will be with you shortly. Would you like a drink while you wait?"

I studied Suzanne's dark gray eyes and laugh lines around her eyes. Suzanne made me feel good and happy to be around her and she made me feel welcomed in this place. When I was hired, she was the person I looked forward to working with the most.

"No, thanks. I'm just going to sit somewhere and wait."

"Alright, hun. Hey, don't be nervous. You'll do just fine!"

"Thanks. I hope."

"Alright, see you later!"

"Thanks."

Suzanne and I nodded to each other and I left the counter. I walked through the restaurant and saw some diners eating a white-yellow cheddar cheesy soup, sandwiches with chicken and some white sauce that I thought was ranch, and what looked like a garden salad that contained the lettuce I thought I got a whiff of. I even saw a family of four, parents with their two sons, share two trays of pepperoni pizza.

What kind of place is this? I need to look at a menu.

I ate a light breakfast this morning. It was only a bowl of oatmeal with a banana. Stepping inside a restaurant didn't help to quell my craving for some food right now. But I kept my focus on this job interview. I needed a job bad. MacKayla spent every penny of our hangout yesterday and I felt so bad about it.

It wasn't until this morning that I gained some gratification within myself because I was taking a proactive step forward in my life. I was trying to become a hard-working citizen like most Americans. More importantly, I was trying to become a hard-working citizen for the Devereauxs to pay them for the hospitality they provided me when I was going to be homeless after my aunt's death.

My aunt's death...

I didn't know what to do with my mission to avenge my aunt's death after I got a job. It was going to be a balance of two priorities that I didn't know how to handle. Maybe I would go hunt for the shapeshifter during the night if I had all shifts for this job during the day? But what if I had night shifts? Will I even have the energy to go hunting this monster down after working a night shift?

Ugh, I don't know!

These thoughts were a distraction in my mind. I tried to wipe them out by thinking of nothing but white space. I thought about the white space I stare at all the time when I stare at my ceiling. That helped…a little.

I sat at a table near the drink station. I saw multiple machines with dispensers for the Coke products. I saw multiple pots of tea, ranging from unsweet and sweet to even a low-calorie sweetened tea. In the distance near the front counter, I saw a red stand filled with copies of to-go menus. I got the idea of looking at a menu to familiarize myself with this place.

I got up from the table and walked all the way up to the front counter to the red stand. I wanted to skim through one before I went through this interview. I grabbed a copy and looked at Suzanne still standing at the counter. She flashed a bright smile at me, and I smiled back at her. It was one more 'You got this!' type of smile from her.

I walked back to my table and sat down to look at the menu. I saw it was separated into multiple categories: soups, salads, sandwiches, pizzas, sides, kid's menu, roundtable items, and drinks. I studied the soup section of the menu first.

"Lobster bisque, shredded chicken tortilla, chicken noodle, chili, loaded cheddar cheese potato…"

Ahh, so that was the soup I smelled.

My eyes gazed towards the sandwich category and I immediately saw the name of the sandwich that had the white sauce in it – Riley's Favorite. A Riley's Favorite sandwich contained chicken, bacon, any choice of cheese customers wanted, and white BBQ sauce.

"White BBQ sauce?"

I thought it was a ranch. There was white BBQ sauce?

A man in his fifties walked up to my table from the back of the restaurant five minutes after I finished looking at the menu. He was a tall, rather chubby man with salt and pepper hair and a white goatee. The man flashed a smile at me as he walked up to my table, although it paled in comparison to the one Suzanne gave me earlier.

"Hello! Are you Ericka?"

"Yes sir, I am."

I got up from my seat and shook the man's hand. His hand almost enveloped mine as he held it and shook it.

"I'm Riley Banks, Jr. It's very nice to meet you."

Wait...what?

"This place is named after you?"

"Yes," he said as he made a slight chuckle. "My father and I started this chain back in 1995. We've since expanded to multiple locations in the Midwest."

"That's amazing. It's a pleasure, sir, and I'm happy to be here!"

"Glad to have you. Please, sit."

We both sat down at the table and I observed that Riley, Jr. was big to the point where the small wooden chair wouldn't sit him entirely.

"So, Ericka. What can you tell me about yourself?"

"Well, my name is Ericka Jones. I'm a senior in high school…"

I lied on my application saying I was still in school. If anybody here knew I didn't even have a GED, my chances of getting would've been zero.

"I'm a hard worker with a passion to learn, train, and excel at any job I get. I have more strengths than weaknesses and I'm ready to contribute to the success of this franchise. Oh, and I'm originally from New York City."

"Fantastic! Tell me about those strengths and weaknesses."

"I consider my strengths to be punctuality, great customer service, quick learner, and I always uphold the high standards of any job I work in. My strengths outweigh my weaknesses, which mainly revolve around me messing up sometimes because I'm not perfect. I also sometimes worry about not doing a good job too often. Other than that, I don't really see any specific, crucial weaknesses."

Riley, Jr. nodded and looked at a piece of paper inside a manila folder, which I inferred was my application. He rubbed the small hairs of his goatee and made a pickle face. Every small non-verbal gesture with his head, hands, and face made me think he was hesitant about giving me a job here as a server. I began to panic. If I couldn't get a job as a server, how the hell am I supposed to get a job anywhere in the future?

"Now, I see here that you don't have any experience.

Which is fine, because you're in high school and being a server doesn't really require much experience. You'll be trained here. However, the majority of people who work here do have some experience and have proven to me they are more than capable of working here. What would you do from day one to prove that you belong at Riley, Jr.'s?"

It took me a few minutes to think of the right answer for this question. I could feel some sweat on top of my forehead while I came up with the best response. I was starting to think that the hardest part of the interview wasn't even here yet. I had to think of something fast. Otherwise, this guy will go to someone else.

"Working at Riley, Jr.'s would be all about serving the customers and helping to build a culture of success. From day one, I would ensure that customers are being served their food on time, to listen to and handle all complaints they have about any meal, to make sure that they're taken care of the minute they walk into the restaurant until the second they leave. But my hard work wouldn't stop there. I'm more than capable of performing all the duties and responsibilities of my job, like cleaning all the tables, filling up cups and drink stations, taking orders, handling roundtable items, and everything else. The essence of what I'm telling you, sir, is that I will adapt and succeed in this restaurant because you need a quick learner and someone who can familiarize themselves with the menu, which I believe is the identity of Riley, Jr.'s."

Once I was done spewing this long answer from my lips, I awaited Riley, Jr.'s reaction. He formed a surprised, amazed look on his face. His eyes widened and he smirked. I didn't know whether to take that as a good sign or bad. I needed him to part his lips and say something to me. Then I would know if I got the job or not.

"Wow. That was a long, impassioned speech."

He laughed a little and looked at my application again. His eyes gazed at the words for a few minutes, which made me think he was stalling the interview to think of a question to ask me. He placed the paper back in the manila folder and lifted his eyes towards me.

"I have one final question to ask you."

I sat up even more straight in my chair in suspense. I waited for the man's final question, which I quipped in my mind might be, "When can you start?"

"Riley, Jr.'s is a community restaurant. As in, there's a sense of community here when customers walk in. We also give drinks on the house to local community heroes, like firefighters, police officers, and doctors. My question is, have you in the past done something good for the community here in Appleton?"

"Yes!" I said as I couldn't contain the excitement on my face.

It was a slam-dunk question and I immediately pulled an answer out of memory lane to finish this interview on a strong note.

"I have volunteered at an animal shelter a couple of times in my sophomore and junior years. I ended up adopting a Pointer I named Speedy. He unfortunately died of a heart murmur. But I would say my time at the animal shelter was a great way for me to help my community."

Riley Jr. nodded and closed the manila folder. He looked at me with a warm smile on his face.

"I can tell you're a smart girl who wants to work and be a contributing member to this restaurant. Congrats, Ericka. You're hired! Can you start tomorrow?"

The smile on my face grew to the point my lips might have stretched out from my cheeks and touched my ears. I gasped and covered my mouth with the palms of my hands, which made Riley, Jr. laugh.

"I've never seen a girl have this reaction to being hired than you."

"Because I'm very excited! Yes, I can start tomorrow!"

"Great! You'll have orientation and training as a server tomorrow. Welcome aboard!"

"Thank you so much!"

I shook Riley, Jr.'s hand as I got up from my seat. I left the restaurant through another exit near the open kitchen of the restaurant. I walked to my car with a feeling of overwhelming joy.

"Hello. How are you, sir?"

"Good, thanks. Can I get a bowl of cheddar loaded potato soup with a side salad and a drink, please? Thank you."

This was my first interaction with a customer at Riley Jr.'s. I stood in front of one out of three touch-screen terminals at the front counter. I poked the buttons for the cheddar loaded potato soup, the garden salad, and a fountain drink. He was charged $21.69 for his order and he paid it with his credit card.

The man looked at me with a mild smile on his face. The wrinkles around his eyes were visible when he smiled and the white mustache on his face curved downwards. He was a lot taller than I was and looked to be in his early fifties.

"Here you go, sir," I said as I handed the man his credit card and the receipt for his order. Enjoy!"

"Thank you!"

"Absolutely!"

The majority of my first day at Riley, Jr.'s were interactions like this one and learning the operations of the restaurant from Suzanne. I couldn't help but be excited when I heard I was working with Suzanne the entire day. Her radiant energy and positive vibes made me feel good to know I was going to work with someone I was comfortable around, especially if I had any questions. I was never afraid around Suzanne to ask any questions I wanted, and she was a complete stranger to me.

Suzanne taught me all the sections of the terminal, which were layers upon layers of grids showing all the foods served at Riley, Jr.'s. The first grid I saw was the list of categories of foods served in the restaurant.

After Suzanne clicked on the sandwich button, I saw a grid listing all the sandwiches made here.

Suzanne clicked on a button with the words "chicken bacon club" and one more grid showed up with the ingredients of the chicken bacon club, along with numerous other toppings any customer wanted to add to the sandwich. On top of the main ingredients was a ribbon of buttons saying 'no,' 'add,' 'side,' 'extra,' 'lite,' and some other stuff.

"Let's say the customer doesn't want any cheese on their chicken bacon club," Suzanne said. "This is how you do it."

Suzanne clicked on the word "no" in the top ribbon and then clicked on the button with the words "provolone cheese." She told me to go to the monitor facing the door where customers would stand, and I saw the order of a chicken bacon club without any cheese on it. Suzanne flashed a smile as I was amazed by how the system worked.

"So, let's say a customer wanted more bacon on their sandwich," I uttered. "I would click on "extra" and then on 'bacon,' correct?"

"That's it! But it's not that simple. The system gets more complicated as you get deeper into it. Let me show you an example."

Suzanne exited out of the sandwich grid and went to the main menu. She clicked on a button called "Take Two."

"The Take Two feature is where a customer wants a

pair of entrees. For example, let's say I'm a customer who wanted a bowl of soup and a half salad."

Suzanne clicked on a button showing the words "chicken noodle." A popup window came up and asked if the customer wanted white bread or whole wheat grain bread with the soup.

"This popup is an example of the system helping you out a little. But let's say that a customer doesn't want a half-sized soup and instead, they want a full soup. You put in the salad they want and the soup they want. Then you see that button that says, "Upgrade to bowl?" You click on that and then the order will have a bowl instead of a cup of soup, which is our half order."

I nodded and was fascinated by how this terminal worked. It seemed so seamless even for me as a beginner and it certainly looked like a system, I would be a professional in after practice and getting used to it.

"You see, earlier when that guy wanted a soup and salad combo, you rang them up as two separate options instead of a Take Two pairing. He wound up paying more when you could've wrung it up as a Take Two and he would've paid about five or so dollars less."

"Oh, oh my goodness. I didn't mean to do that."

"It's okay! It's your first day. It looks like you can get the hang of it in a few days. Some have a problem with this that lasts for weeks. Then they have to be retrained on it and go through the grids all over again. Besides, there are some employees who've been here for years that still make mistakes. You'll get used to it and master it eventually!"

"I hope so."

"Oh, one more thing before we move on to something else. Always ask the customer if they want a whole sandwich instead of half. The Take Two feature has a whole sandwich option."

"Got it."

"Alright. Let's move on to roundtable."

I followed Suzanne to the back of the kitchen, where we moved past the dishwashing station to a walk-in refrigerator. It had white stucco, heavy duty and galvanized steel doors that did its job of keeping the cooler sealed. I saw a thermometer next to the door and its needle was pointed at the number thirty-three.

Suzanne grabbed the metal handle of the door and pulled hard on it. We both went into the fridge and I saw racks upon racks of ingredients for the food at Riley, Jr.'s. I saw all types of meats and cheeses, shredded, sliced, and pulled, all in labeled containers and jars. I even saw trays of chicken, steak, and shrimp being held inside a multi-layered rack with wheels.

"For roundtable items, we get them from the bottom rack here."

Suzanne pointed to the bottom shelf of the rack that was immediately to our left when we first walked in. I saw containers of cherry peppers, jalapenos, capers, lemons, parmesan cheese, olives, garlic, and banana peppers. It was like being in a library of food with everything labeled and indexed.

"Whenever we need roundtable items filled up

front, we come to the walk-in fridge and grab the items from here, okay?"

"Sounds good!"

Suzanne smiled and grabbed the containers of parmesan cheese, lemons, and capers. She told me to grab the olives and garlic. I did as she told me and followed her to the other part of the back room. The kitchen was open, and the back room acted as a supplier to the cooks who did their magic in the adjoining kitchen.

We both went to a shelf that had small lids and small, black portion cups. Suzanne put the containers she was holding down on a counter underneath the shelf and pointed towards the lids and cups.

"The majority of the roundtable items we fill up at the roundtable station will be filled up in these cups. I say a majority because only two items aren't filled up in these cups: lemons and croutons, which I'll show you where they are up front. Got it, Ericka?"

"Yes, ma'am."

"Alright, so lemons and croutons are filled up in different-sized containers. Croutons are filled up in these cups right here."

Suzanne pointed to a bag of two-ounce polystyrene cups and the lids that belonged to them. She then told me that the lemons belonged in sixteen-ounce polystyrene cups with bigger lids because the wedges were bigger.

"So now that you know about roundtable items and how to do them, and with how familiar you've gotten to the terminals, let's fill up all these items and then you'll be done for the day."

"Thank you so much. You have no idea how much your guidance will help me succeed in this job, Suzanne. I really appreciate it."

"No problem, honey."

I came back home and immediately went to the bathroom. I felt an emergency on my way here and I couldn't wait to just release it all. I looked in the mirror after I was done and I washed my hand, seeing the uniform and cap I wore on my head. The uniform was just a restaurant shirt and jeans. I looked at the cap and saw my name on it. I felt proud of myself for getting this job and becoming a money-earning member of the Devereauxs. I couldn't wait to start being independent and start to pay them back for their hospitality.

I washed my hands and dried them up before I walked to my bedroom. I was scared to fuck when I saw MacKayla jump out of her bedroom with excitement.

"Geez, MacKayla! What the hell?"

"Sorry, I didn't know you were such a wuss. Hillary wants to chat with us. Come on, let's go in my bedroom."

MacKayla hurried to her room and I followed slowly behind. She hopped on her bed and patted the side of it right next to her, motioning for me to sit there with her. I took off my cap and unrolled my hair from the scrunchy it's been wrapped in all day. It felt good to loosen up in the comfort of home and just relax on my bed with my two best friends. MacKayla had her laptop open on Skype and was ready to press the button to talk to Hillary.

MacKayla pressed it and we waited on Hillary to open her virtual window. Hillary came live on the Skype window and she couldn't contain her happiness when saw MacKayla and I right next to each other waving at her. She was in a much better mood than the last time we saw her, probably because Chad was in her life after moving to Virginia. A cheerful smile appeared on her face that was as bright as the sunlight that shined through her room.

"Oh my gosh! How are my two beautiful girls doing?" she asked.

"We're good!" MacKayla shouted. "We have a lot to talk about. But first, how are you doing?"

"I'm doing so good. I've got a boyfriend in my life and I've finally adjusted to Virginia. I have a job working at Staples while I'm trying to finish this senior year already."

"Yay, that's amazing!" I said.

"How are you guys doing?" Hillary asked. "Especially you, Ericka. How are you, beautiful?"

"I'm doing well for myself."

"Ericka here has a job now," MacKayla intervened. "She's a 'responsible,' 'mature' human being now."

"Oh, my goodness," Hillary remarked. "That's amazing."

"Why are you using air quotes?"

"Because I want to."

"Anyways, MacKayla is right. You can see the company shirt I'm wearing. I'm working at a restaurant called Riley, Jr.'s. It sells sandwiches, soups, salads, pizza –"

"OMG, stop talking," Hillary said. "You're making me so hungry right now. I can never ever work at restaurants. I would just devour every food I served to those people. Won't you be afraid of getting mouth water all the time just smelling and looking at that food?"

"No. I'm more worried about the money, not the food. I'm trying to get paid and save up for bigger things in the future."

"Like?"

"I don't know. Just stuff."

Hillary nodded with a smile on her face that said 'Yeah, right. Sure. Bigger things.'

"Anyways, I'm glad you got a job, babe. I'm happy for you."

"Thanks."

"Yeah, I'm especially happy for her after that jerk wad Derek treated her so horribly."

"MacKayla!"

"What? You have to tell Hillary what happened."

A look of concern grew on Hillary's face. It's like

she feared Derek would do physical harm to me and assumed the worst immediately.

"Oh my gosh, what happened between you and Derek? Did he hurt you?"

"No, of course not. We just got into an argument where he said some awful things. I don't want to talk about it."

"Well, too bad because I want to know," Hillary said.

"Let MacKayla tell you. But talking about this whole thing will just make me remember that night all over again."

MacKayla looked at me with an expression of disappointment and shook her head. She sighed before looking at Hillary through the screen of her laptop.

"I'll tell you what happened, Hill. The assclown had the nerves to be a sore loser after Ericka beat him at bowling. He cussed and yelled at her and even said that her parents would be proud of raising a cheater like her."

Hillary gasped in response to what MacKayla told her. She placed her hands on her wide gaping lips and looked at MacKayla and I with the widest eyes we'd ever seen from her.

"Oh my gosh! He disrespect your parents? That's awful, honey. I'm so sorry."

"We didn't even need to talk about it in the first place, you know? I was happy to just forget about it."

"No, why would you want to hide this from me?"

"It's what she did to me," MacKayla said, causing me

to roll my eyes at her. "She kept it from me for *six days*, just bottled up inside her."

"Look enough, alright? I just got back from work and I'm feeling a little tired."

"I'm sorry, honey. You don't need that lowlife and loser in your life. I hope you're done with him."

I nodded and looked at my friends with an expression of sadness. MacKayla rubbed my back and I felt somewhat comfortable from what seemed like an attempt at an apology.

"I should go," Hillary said. "I have an errand to run. We'll talk later?"

"Absolutely!" MacKayla said.

"Sounds good, Hill."

"Alright, bye for now."

We bade Hillary goodbye and MacKayla closed her laptop. She looked at me with my head bowed down to my side and avoided her gaze. She felt bad for rehashing the incident between Derek and me. So, she grabbed me and hugged me, rubbing my back and hair.

"I'm sorry, Ericka. Hillary had a right to know. Forgive me?"

I reached my hands out and wrapped them around my best friend.

"You know I always do."

I sighed as I absorbed the comfort given to me by MacKayla. I smiled knowing I could always turn to her for comfort now that Derek was out of my life. For good.

15

It was five in the afternoon and I still had my work clothes on. I was at the park with a sweater pulled close to my chest because it was forty-five degrees out. My shift at Riley, Jr.'s was over, and I came here to unwind. I grabbed a bag of breadcrumbs and spread them on the floor to feed the birds. Once I did that, I pulled out my phone and pressed my thumb against the music app.

I pulled all my songs to listen to, starting with a favorite Taylor Swift song I loved so much – *Bad Blood*. I pushed my phone back into my pocket and readjusted the headphones in my ears, so they fit better. While I listened to my songs and saw the birds have a free-for-all melee for the bread, I couldn't help but think about him.

I needed a plan to fight and kill the shapeshifter to avenge Aunt Carrie. But with Derek no longer in the picture, it was impossible for me to come up with a plan to fight this monster. Even though I hated Derek with all my guts for lying to me and making me look stupid, I was just a mortal girl.

Here I was trying to draw up a plan to battle a supernatural monster when I had all the weaknesses of the world as a human. The odds were stacked against me so high I couldn't see the top of the stack. At least when Derek was by my side, I had a werewolf who would fight with me. I had the help of another super-natural monster who used its powers to weaken the monster I was so trying to exterminate.

Now I was all alone. Maybe I was just shutting Derek out of my life because I was so mad at him for lying to me. But more importantly, I was mad at myself for believing him when I had one of the best intuitions of any female in this world. I felt humiliated and dumb instead for taking the word of a werewolf over my own instincts.

Maybe I was being too harsh on him. I mean, being a wolf must mean watching your back 24/7 from humans. Maybe he lied to me because he was afraid, I would expose him, and he would be hunted down by a human lynch mob and killed or something. I did threaten him with it, and I must've scared him into lying to me. All these maybes were clouding my head. I had so much on my mind.

I sat on the bench troubled over what plan or step of action I would take to fight the shapeshifter alone. Things became worse when I suddenly remembered the Latin phrases that the shifter shouted, which were some hidden supernatural powers it had. The shifter threw me on the ground without touching me.

On top of that, the shifter made me so frozen and so immobile I could barely move anything. All from these Latin phrases. How on earth was I supposed to battle the shifter now that my brain has suddenly remembered these things? Will I even come up with a plan for killing the shifter now that I know some of its hidden powers?

I couldn't help but become emotional. I paused the music on my phone and turned it off. I pushed it back into my pocket with anger and frustration. I even took the bag of crumbs from out of my sweater and threw them on the ground in pure rage. I saw multiple birds fighting for the bag and its contents before I placed my hands over my eyes and started crying.

I felt like I was back to square one with this whole mission. I felt as lost as when I first saw the shifter and didn't know what it was before I discovered the existence of monsters in this world. Should I contact Derek and team up with him again to fight against the shifter and tell him about those Latin phrases from the shifter? Doing so meant giving him a pass for what he did to me and I wasn't ready to forgive him.

At the same time, he was a valuable resource to me about the world of the supernatural. No one else knew about monsters other than other monsters. I needed something or someone so bad to help me with my mission, but I wasn't ready to welcome Derek back into my life yet.

"Ericka? Oh my gosh, what's wrong?"

I heard a worried voice to my right side. It was high-pitched in tone and I knew I heard it before. I wiped some tears away before I looked at the person. It was a girl with light brown hair and a recognizable flower bomb scent that emitted from her body.

"Maisy? What are you doing here?"

I haven't seen Maisy since last Fall when I was still enrolled at Angelwood for my senior year. It's been a while since I almost forgot I had her as a friend. Maisy sat down next to me and started to rub my back.

"I always take a walk through this park whenever I feel like it. First, let me just say how sorry I am for your aunt's...death. I heard about it on the news, and I wanted to see you so bad, but I didn't know if you still lived at your aunt's house after what happened or where you live now. So, I'm really glad I'm with you now."

"Thanks."

"Why are you sitting here in the park crying? Are you still grieving the death of your aunt? I'm so sorry if you are."

"No, it's not that. It's something else."

"Well, what is it? You can tell me anything. I'm here for you."

She rubbed my back more and moved closer towards me. I wiped a few tears away from my face and contemplated whether I should tell her the same lie I told MacKayla or a new lie since MacKayla and Maisy don't spoke all the time anymore. She wouldn't find out from MacKayla about what I said to MacKayla, but I just thought I'd play it safe and keep my story consistent.

"There's this guy named Derek. We were friends for a brief period of time, and we met in the cafeteria at Angelwood. We became good friends. Derek and I went bowling a week ago and I beat him. He was a jerk afterwards and acted like a sore loser."

"What did he do? I hope he didn't physically attack you or anything. You need to get the police involved if he did."

"No, no. He didn't do anything like that. He just yelled and cursed at me, and I yelled and cursed at him. He then disrespected my dead parents."

"What?"

"Yeah."

I looked at Maisy and saw her mouth was wide open. I looked away from her and lowered my head down to look at the bread crumb remains on the ground after the birds all disappeared.

"You're crying over a guy who's not worth it! If you're telling me that you're sitting here in this park crying because of some jackass, then you don't need to! You don't need a scum of the earth like that in your life to make you cry and cause you sorrow and pain. He's not worth it, Ericka. Please tell me this guy is out of your life."

"Well yeah. I told him I didn't want to see his face again and I told him to lose all contact with me."

"Good. I'm glad. I can't believe this guy would act like a sore loser. What did he say to you?"

"He accused me of cheating and told me I was using a lighter ball. I was like, 'Yeah because I'm smaller than you.' I could go into detail about it, but I won't. I just want to move on from the situation and forget about it. Forget about Derek, too."

Maisy nodded and continued to rub my back. She smiled and placed my head on her shoulders, after which she gave me a hug and I embraced her back.

"I'm so sorry this happened to you."

"Thanks, Maisy."

The embrace between us ended and I managed to smile mildly at her.

"So, what's going on with you? Tell me about you. What have you been doing in your life since the last time I saw you?"

Maisy made a look of excitement on her face as she sat up on the bench right next to me.

"So, there's this guy I'm courting, and his name is Nathan. I met him in December, and we've been dating since."

"Oh, my goodness!" I said with a big smile on my face and widened my eyes. "That's great, Maisy. I'm happy for you."

"Thanks, hun. He goes to Angelwood and we see each other there all the time! Isn't that amazing?"

"It really is. I'm happy for you."

"Well, what about you? Anything good in your life happened lately?"

"Umm…I got a job at Riley, Jr.'s –"

Maisy gasped and covered her mouth.

"What?"

"That's my favorite restaurant! I always try to go there! Oh my gosh, they have the most amazing pizzas ever. And their sandwiches are so warm and toasted, they're so good."

"Awesome! So, I'll see you there from time to time?"

"Yes, of course!"

"Maybe it'll be my treat."

Maisy shook her head and looked at me with a serious expression.

"No, you absolutely won't. It'll be my treat."

"Oh, come on. It was your treat the last time we went to the movies. I have a job now. Let me repay the favor. Come on, please."

It was then that Maisy sighed mildly and looked at me with a cute smile. I could even see a little twinkle in her eyes from when the sun's rays hit her face at an angle that caused the whole right side of her face to shine bright.

"Okay, fine. If you insist."

"Great! I look forward to it!"

Maisy took out her phone and looked at it briefly to see the time. She placed it back in and turned her gaze towards me.

"I have to go home. I'll see you and talk to you later, alright? You can text me whenever you want. I'm here for you."

"You're sweet. Thanks, Maisy."

Maisy wrapped her arms around me and mine around hers. I felt the heat of her head when the sun shined on it behind her. The strands of her long brown hair were as warm and toasty as the sandwiches she described.

"Stay strong, okay? Keep your head up and don't cry over anybody who doesn't deserve it."

"Okay. Thanks, hun."

"You got it, Ericka."

Maisy let me go and walked away from me, waving at me as she went further in the distance. I remained sitting on the bench and stared at the people in the landscape in front of me. I saw couples walking, owners walking their dogs, and birds wolfing down seeds being thrown at them from the pale, wrinkled hands of a woman with short, curly gray hair.

16

I spent most of the day in my room drawing up a plan to defeat the shapeshifter. I mean, how hard could it be? It was a humanoid shapeshifter. All I had to do was find its heart and plunge my long, *silver* machete through it, which had to be in its chest... Except I got the nagging feeling it wasn't the case.

It couldn't be that easy. It was a monster after all, not a human with a normal heart or chest for that matter. I even began to think that maybe shapeshifters didn't have a heart, that they were powered by super-natural fuel or something.

I wish I had Bart Ramsay's book.

My only plan of action was to try and stab the shapeshifter everywhere I could to see if I penetrate its heart somewhere in its body...if it had a heart. I also thought about decapitation as another possible way to end the shifter's life once and for all. But then, an idea came to mind. It was an epiphany I never thought of before.

I couldn't act on it immediately because my phone buzzed with so many message notifications. I opened up my phone and saw I got three texts from Derek. I opened my phone and I looked at all three messages.

Derek: Ericka, it's been days since you've discovered my secret. It's been days and you haven't talked to me. Please allow me to talk to you.

Derek: I messed up so bad and I reaalllyyyy feel bad for it. There's no excuse for betraying your trust and your friendship and I feel awful for it. Please let me explain to you why I lied to you about Josh and being a werewolf.

Derek: I was afraid to lose you. You mean so much to me, Ericka. I was afraid if you knew who I was, you'd never talk to me and be anywhere near me. Please, let's just talk and I'll give you every reason why you shouldn't be afraid of me.

I closed my phone and tossed it to the side. I felt so bad for the way I've shut him out like this after doing so much for me. But I needed guys in my life who were honest with me and confessed to me the skeletons in their closet. Derek took advantage of my naivety about the world of the supernatural and made me look stupid. I won't fall for that trap twice. But all the times he took care of me at his cabin came flooding back to my mind. He was so sweet to do that.

I dealt with a huge headache from my feelings about Derek. I knew he would be agonized by the fact that I read his messages and ignored them, since he would see on the text messaging app that I read his messages. Do I forgive him for lying to me and move on because of all the kind and caring things he did for me? Or do I just continue slapping him with silent treatment as a small punishment for lying from the tips of his lips? Maybe I would consider doing the first option in due time.

But I didn't think about this pair of burning questions anymore for the night because I had an epiphany involving Derek. More specifically, it involved that show he watched, *Supernatural*. I opened my laptop and went on the wiki page of the show. The second I opened it; I saw pictures of four flaming hot, gorgeous dudes who I thought were the main characters of the show.

I took a brief second to study their appearance, but what I thought was a brief second turned into like five minutes…

Damn, they're hot. But focus girl!

I got rid of my distraction and typed the word "shapeshifter" in the search bar of the *Supernatural* wiki page. I went to the page on shapeshifters and immediately saw a table of contents and one of the sections was "weaknesses." I clicked on that section and saw silver and iridium as some of the weaknesses for shapeshifters, which Derek already told me about.

But then I saw things like heart extraction, explosions, and decapitation as other ways to weaken or kill a shifter. I needed to find its heart first to extract it and destroy it. I didn't know how to get my hands on any bombs or explosives to blow the shifter to pieces. I didn't know how to make one and if I was seen trying to make one or appear with one anywhere in town, I would land in prison for the rest of my life.

It was bad enough that I had to be careful to hide the silver machete Derek gave me in the trunk of my car. No one would ever know it was there. Explosions were definitely not an option. But I could decapitate the shapeshifter. That was in my thought process earlier and *Supernatural* confirmed it.

So now my plan was finding and extracting the heart of the shapeshifter by stabbing it anywhere and everywhere in its body to find the heart, starting with its chest. I could also do it the easy way and kill the SOB by decapitation. I would do it all using my silver machete.

Great!

I still got the feeling that I should be equipped with more weapons than a machete, though. I needed a weapon made out of iridium. I didn't have that and I sure as hell wasn't going to get it from Derek. Then I thought about getting a silver necklace or something, to weaken the shifter if it got close to me. I could burn its skin with it or something.

I still had one more piece of the puzzle to figure out. I had a plan of action and even thought of the weapons to use against the shifter. But I still needed to know how to negate the effects of those Latin phrases the shifter used against me. I was beginning to think they were some types of magic spells. The idea of a shapeshifter with knowledge of magic frightened me and I needed to go somewhere for help, as well as an iridium weapon and a silver pendant.

I exited out of the *Supernatural* page and opened another tab. I thought about where to go for magic, a place with knowledge about magic, both white and dark. I typed up the question 'Where can I go to learn about magic?' I got no relevant answers but something helpful came up, nonetheless.

A list of magic metaphysical supply shops came up and I learned there was one in Appleton named The Magic Witches' Bazaar. I made up my mind to go to this place, thinking it was like a library for people who knew about magic.

The next day, after my shift at Riley, Jr.'s ended, I made a secret trip to The Magic Witches' Bazaar. It was a small boutique store and the first sight I saw was of numerous shelves containing different bottles and jars with herbs, incense, strange looking rocks and jewelry, oils, and plants.

The creepiest part of the store was the section of shelves containing several statues, idols of monsters and creatures with heads different from their bodies, skulls, Egyptian and foreign artifacts, and even the most horrifying-looking dolls I've ever seen in my life, which gave me the chills. I finally saw candles, bowls, bells, and other things that could be placed on a table or altar of some sort.

I couldn't help but smell the fragrance dominant inside the store. It was an incense of some sort and the smell were of a combination of berries and citrusy fruit. At least the smell calmed my nerves from all the dreadful artifacts in this shop and the ominous pale décor. I walked up to the front counter and saw a bell that I pressed to let whoever worked here know that I was there.

A wooden bead curtain leading to a back room opened and a woman who looked to be in her fifties walked through it. She was a bit taller than I am and had long, raven dark hair that was thinning, which made me guess she was almost in her sixties. The woman had light gray eyes and wore eye liner around them. The woman looked at me with a wide smile on her face along with squinted eyes.

"Hello, dear. How may I help you?"

"Hi. Yes, umm…"

I didn't know how to tell why I came to this shop. How do I tell this lady that I was here looking for a way to negate the magic spells of a shapeshifter? Did she even know about monsters at all, let alone shapeshifters? Maybe her shop was just for props and gags, not actual magic. How do I talk to this lady?

Oh, gosh. Pull it together and just do it.

"I really don't know how to tell you this, but I'm not really here to buy anything. I came for help about magic."

The woman looked at me with intrigue in her eyes. She raised her head and nodded, with the smile on her face fading away. The lady squinted her eyes at me, which made me nervous.

"What type of help?"

I was getting flustered with her. There was no easy way to tell her about my situation, so I just decided to say it bluntly. I don't care if she thinks I'm a lunatic. I just need someone to hear me and help me because it won't be Derek, at least not right now.

"I need your help in a battle I'm waging against a shapeshifter. It's a monster that has the ability to shift into any appearance like its name says. Before you say anything, I need to tell you that monsters exist. I know this sounds strange and you might think I'm a nut, but monsters are real. A shapeshifter killed my aunt, and it was going to kill me when I was saved by a werewolf. I know this sounds crazy, but it's true. Monsters are real."

The woman's eyes widened, and she looked at me with more curiosity than ever. She raised her head again and nodded, while the gaze of her eyes turned somewhere else. Then, the smile on her face returned and she started laughing. I knew she thought I was insane. I felt so embarrassed, like I made a fool out of myself in front of a random stranger. My cheeks flushed red, and I had a look of extreme humiliation on my face before she stopped and looked back at me.

"Oh, dear. I know the monsters are real."

I looked up at her with a look of surprise.

"Wait, what?"

"Yes, darling. I know monsters are real. You're not crazy at all. In fact, I'm actually surprised that *you* know about monsters. Normal humans think this is all fictional. I'm sorry I laughed and made you think you were crazy. But I know monsters are real. After all, I was trying to be one of them."

The look of utter surprise turned into one of horrified confusion. *Tried to be a monster?*

"Let me explain. But first, my name is Cassandra. What's yours, dear?"

She reached her hand out to me like she wanted to shake it. I reached my hand out to her and she wrapped both her hands around mine. It was then that I started to feel comfortable around this lady as her hands provided me with some unexpected warmth. But I was still scared and confused as hell about what she said.

"Ericka."

"Lovely name."

She let go of my hand and retracted it with a nervous look on my face.

"Calm down, Ericka. I sense an awful feeling of trepidation coming from you. I'm not going to harm you. I'm going to help you."

"What do you mean you were trying to be a monster?"

Cassandra nodded and grabbed a stool from behind her. She sat on the counter and adjusted herself on the seat. She clutched her hands together and placed them on top of the counter before looking at me with a luke-warm, mild smile.

"When I was in my twenties, I enrolled in a witch academy. I tried to be a white witch. I guess since you know about monsters, you know there are two types of witches – black and white."

"What? No, I didn't!"

"Huh…alright then. White witches are the good, pure ones who use magic for good. Dark, black witches corrupt magic and use it for evil. All witches, whether good or evil, become witches through secret academies located all throughout the world. But they can also degrade the minds of witches, which is what differentiates the good ones from the evil ones."

I was shocked to hear this revelation, yet so empowered that I knew about it. No one else could know about this.

"I promise I won't tell anyone what you just said. In case you make me swear secrecy."

"Smart girl."

"You tried to be a white witch?"

"Yes dear, but I was kicked out. I was deemed insufficiently ready to handle the powers of magic. So, I came here and opened up this beauty. Not all men and women who want to learn witchcraft graduate from those academies. And not all those who are kicked out are black witches, either."

I nodded and tried to absorb what Cassandra told me. I felt so good and empowered inside to learn about witches. The more knowledge I knew, the stronger I felt. I was especially happy since I thought to myself that Cassandra would be my new source for information about the supernatural world. I could ditch Derek to the curb without thinking about how I'm going to deal with the shapeshifter without him.

"So how did you keep up with magic after you were kicked out?"

Cassandra cracked a devious smile on her face and her eyes squinted once again.

"Unbeknownst to the headmasters, I snuck some books from the academy's library. They're in the back room but I don't really want to show them to you."

"That's fine," I said with a confident nod. "I'm just here for help to deal with this shapeshifter that happens to know magic. It said some Latin phrases and the next thing I knew; I was thrown to the ground from a wave of its hands, and I was frozen in place with another motion of its hands."

Cassandra donned a serious look on her face and nodded. She grabbed a notepad and paper and wrote down some Latin words. Cassandra then slid the notepad towards me.

"Are those the words you heard?"

I looked at the paper and saw the words *mittent* and *rigescunt indutae*, which lead to a shocked expression in my eyes.

"Yes! Oh my gosh, those are it! What are they?"

"The first one is a telekinesis spell. The other one is biokinesis. Those two spells are mainly from black magic."

"What are those words you just said?"

Cassandra chuckled a little.

"Telekinesis is the ability to move objects or exert force on objects without actual contact. Biokinesis is the ability to manipulate life forms and their physical bodies. That's how the shifter was able to throw you to the ground without touching you and freezing your entire body."

I was terrified to learn this. I placed the notepad on the table and shook my head in utter disbelief. Not only was I dealing with a shapeshifter, but the black witch that was supplying it with these dark magic spells. I placed my hands on my mouth and started to breathe heavier than usual. Next thing I knew, Cassandra placed her arms around me and tried to comfort me.

"It's alright, sweetie. Just calm down. I know this is all news to you. But I'm here to help. I have a basic negation spell that you can use."

I turned to face Cassandra and looked deep into her eyes, serious as ever.

"Will it work?"

"I can't give you my word it'll be a 100% foolproof. It's somewhat effective and it's what you need, though. But there's one more thing you need to know."

"What's that?"

"Witch spells can't be recited by human beings. Let's just say monsters are more adaptable to the harmful effects of magic but humans aren't. You'll need to wear a magic talisman that protects you from the physical toll that comes with casting magic spells."

"Wait, what physical toll? What harmful effects?"

"If you cast witch spells without the protection of a talisman, you'll suffer from things like nose bleeds, a drain of energy, severe headaches, your body will be really weak, those kinds of things. I've seen people even suffer a heart attack and die from trying to cast a magic spell without a talisman."

"Oh my gosh," I said as I covered my mouth.

Cassandra nodded before she said, "I'll be right back with the negation spell you need and a talisman, dear. I'll write the spell down on a piece of paper for you."

"Wait, I have a question."

Cassandra stood stationary behind the counter and looked at me with wide open, curious eyes.

"Will the talisman protect me from the shapeshifter's spells that it casts on me?"

"Unfortunately no, dear. The talisman only protect you from the side effects of magic when you perform it. I'm afraid I don't have any talisman that does what you're referring to."

I nodded and thanked Cassandra for her help and for not thinking I was insane. She went to the back and retrieved the spell along with a diamond-shaped, silver, sharp-edged talisman. There were a bunch of witch and wiccan symbols carved on its surface, like various moons, a bunch of stars, weird-shaped crosses, and what looked like Egyptian hieroglyphs.

"You'll need to recite the negation spell before going

to battle with the shapeshifter. And that talisman is very effective."

I took my eyes off of it and placed it around my neck before I looked at Cassandra with a smile.

"I can't thank you enough for helping me out. I really appreciate it."

"I bid you farewell, dear."

"Bye for now," I said as I walked out of Cassandra's shop.

17

Oh my gosh! Why hasn't she responded to my messages?!

I haven't slept peacefully the last few days. The scene where I was lying on the ground healing from an injury while Ericka witnessed it replayed in my mind constantly. My mind was adding insult to injury. I felt like I was kicking myself while I was already down. I couldn't even make breakfast today and the couple of days prior when I did eat, I didn't enjoy the taste of anything.

She can't be that cold-hearted. Ericka was still angry at me; I knew that much. But surely, she must be thinking about all the good I've done for her. I've been nothing but kind to her. I trained her how to fight with her hands and use weapons against the shapeshifter. I've saved her from the damn shifter every time she fought it.

Ericka had to be conflicted. She had to be debating

in her mind whether or not to forgive me based on everything I've done for her. I just wish the lie I told her wouldn't be dominating her thought process. But I guess she was going to find out in the end. Ericka was going to learn the truth about me eventually, but I didn't want it to be like that. The hurt look on her face when she found out I was a werewolf also played in my mind.

It was then that I got off my couch. I had to figure out a way to get her back, but how? I don't know where she lives so I can't go there. Even if I knew and did just that, she would get the police involved and I didn't want any attention. She's out of school so I can't confront her there. I wonder if she has a job. I would go there but she could be working anywhere in the city if that was the case.

My calls and text messages were certainly not working because she may have blocked me. I'm over here being frantic as hell wondering whether or not she saw them.

Fuck! What do I do now?

I heard a knock on my door.

Ugh, what now?

I walked to the cabin door with every footstep I took being loud from the bottom of my sneakers and filled with irritation. I opened the door and swung it open with a furious motion. I saw Frank standing in the door with a serious look on his face.

"What do you want, Frank?"

"I came here with some troubling news. The pack

just repelled an attack on you by a small group of wolves which Jason thinks belong to a pack led by an alpha named Leon. Jason thinks that he's trying to take over the Appleton territory since it's unoccupied."

"Why is that?"

"Why it's unoccupied? I don't know. We just moved here to help you. Yet your uncle already has a theory that the former alpha of the territory left because his numbers were dwindling, and he moved away to find new wolves to recruit. We think Leon is trying to expand or something. But your uncle won't let that happen. He's drawing up a plan to repel Leon's pack. I imagine there's going to be a war between us and Leon's pack."

I nodded and looked away from Frank. I couldn't care less what was happening with my uncle and his pack right now. I was thinking only about Ericka and how to win her back. I stayed for a few seconds thinking about her, frozen in my place and not giving any thought to the world around me. It was then I heard Frank's fingers snap in front of my face.

"Hello, Earth to Derek."

I snapped out of it and looked at Frank with an annoyed expression.

"What?"

"I asked if you'll join your uncle in fighting against Leon. He'll count on it."

"Look, I don't have time to talk about this right now. I have something to take care of first. Thanks for letting me know. Tell my uncle that I appreciate his help and that I'll contact him soon."

"Alright. See you later."

"Bye."

I closed the door in Frank's face and went back to my living room. I just said those things to get Frank out of my face. I was too concentrated on Ericka to even fathom giving my uncle a call. I sat back down on the couch and released a big sigh. I had to think of a way to get Ericka to forgive me so we can return to our friendship. I just don't know how I'll see her again unless she's in the forest fighting the shapeshifter again.

18

I t was dead at night and I was all alone in the forest. I felt more confident this time around as I looked for the shapeshifter. I had my silver machete and a new weapon. I also had a special-made iridium sickle in my other hand. I bought both of these things from Cassandra at her store. She had the sickle as part of a small but very secret cache of weapons in the back of her store.

The most effective weapons I had, though, were the negation spell and the magic talisman Cassandra gave me. I recited the Latin incantation before I stepped foot on the soil of the forest. If the shifter decided to use its dark magic against me, I was confident it would meet its match. I was going to avenge my aunt tonight and end this thing once and for all.

I prowled through the forest looking for the shifter. My heartbeat was abnormal, and I got nervous as I smelled the fresh dew and minty smell of the forest trees. I looked all around me and the sight of endless trees danced in my eyes. I rubbed them so I wouldn't get dazed and so my vision would be as clear as possible.

Just like every time I came to this forest, my nerves jumped when I heard even the smallest sound. I was vigilant about any possible ambush by the shifter and I wasn't going to let it have an advantage over me. I was going to end its life tonight, one way or the other, and I couldn't allow myself any room for mistakes.

I came across a small clearing and it gave me a small bit of relief. At least in the clearing, everything was right in front of me, and I wasn't as vulnerable to a surprise attack by the shapeshifter. But no sooner had I gotten to the clearing that I saw something on the ground. They were footprints.

I studied the footprints closely and saw they were human footprints. I looked around the footprints and saw more of them. I didn't know if they truly belonged to a human or the shapeshifter. Maybe it was a recent victim of the shifter. All I inferred was that these footprints may have something to do with the monster and they could possibly lead me to it.

I followed the footprints as a clue to the shifter's whereabouts. I needed something to help me find this God-forsaken monster before I got lost in the woods and I wouldn't find a way out. I was hellbent on finding it and massacring life out of it. I followed every footprint along the path, balancing my gaze between the prints and what was in front of me.

The further I went along this trail and the more I studied the footprints, I noticed that they started to fade. It wasn't until I arrived at a random tree that the trail ceased, and I no longer saw any footprints. I was expecting to see a dead body if it was a human but... nothing. I saw nothing. I looked at the tree for more clues and I got what I looked for. Some of the bark had scratches on it.

I probed the bark closely and saw that the marks looked like they came from claws. In an instant, I knew it was the shifter. Or it could have been Derek. But how can he climb the tree in wolf form? The footprints made sense since they stopped at the tree. Maybe he changed to wolf form at the point the path stops and climbed onto the tree. But if that were the case, I would've seen paw prints right where the human prints ended.

I didn't have any more time to think about the matter because I was interrupted. I heard branches and leaves shaking. I froze in my place with my weapons ready at hand. The branches and leaves that I heard moving were coming directly from above me. They belonged to the tree in front of me.

I didn't want to look up, but I wanted to see what made the tree branches and leaves shake. I could've been scared for nothing. It might have been a squirrel or a raccoon, or another innocent animal. But given that some heavy parts of the tree moved, I doubted it was a small animal who did it. No, this was a large creature.

The shaking of the tree leaves and branches then got louder, like whatever was started to descend the tree…and get closer to me. I built up the courage and looked up at the tree after I closed my eyes and counted down from three. I tilted my head up and I saw it lunging at me from the top of a tree branch.

The shifter had my appearance and it showed me its prickly teeth as it swooped down from the tree. I couldn't duck out of the way in time and the monster fell on top of me. I lost my grip over the machete after feeling the impact of the shifter landing on top of me. I thought quickly and I took my necklace as the shifter adjusted itself on top of me.

With my silver talisman in hand, I stabbed the shifter in its eyes, causing some type of black ooze to stream down its face while a small amount of steam rose from its eyes from the burning sensation of the silver. Its loud, piercing scream made my ears deaf, and I couldn't handle it anymore.

I took my necklace away from the shifter's eye and forced it to get off me. It gripped its eye and continued to scream in pain. I took the opportunity to locate my machete and ran to it immediately. I took it in my hand as the shifter turned around and looked at me. I could see a hole in its eye that was starting to self-heal.

I attacked the shifter with no time to waste and started to swing my machete and iridium sickle across its entire body. All I saw was black, thick blood along with hot steam coming from the shifter's skin. It writhed in pain and screamed immensely. But I felt a moment of victory when I brought the shifter to its knees.

I dropped the sickle to the ground while the monster was on its knees and aimed my machete at the shifter's chest. I ran towards it and plunged the machete into its chest, thinking about its heart being there. The monster froze in place and looked up at the sky in deep pain. I thought at that moment that I achieved victory and killed the shifter. I even began to smell victory.

What I smelled, however, was the burning skin of the shapeshifter from the chest wound I caused it. I watched in horror as the shapeshifter got up from the ground, although with much pain and blood still oozing out of it. Its eye healed entirely as it looked at me with fire in its eyes and rage burning in its guts.

The shifter's heart was not in its chest. My first instinct was right. The shapeshifter ejected my machete from its chest, screaming in pain as it gripped the silver blade in its hands and aggravating its own wound while getting the blade out in its entirety. I watched in horror while closing my ears to block the loud sound of the shifter's scream.

The shapeshifter dropped my machete on the ground immediately as the wound in its chest started to slowly, but gradually, self-heal. It reached it hands out to the machete and yelled the word *calor*. My machete levitated off the ground as the shifter motioned for it to rise from the ground.

I looked at my machete and I saw the silver beginning to melt. My eyes widened and I covered my mouth to contain any screams that might come out. I was in disbelief as I saw my primary weapon, which was not supposed to burn or melt in any way, was no longer useful and laid on the ground in a pile of liqui-fied silver. The machete's handle laid to the side, nothing more than a useless piece of crap.

"Nooo!"

I watched in internal agony as my dad's machete lied on the ground, disintegrated. The shifter completely self-healed from any stab and scratch marks I made on its body while I wasted my one chance of weakening it long enough to kill it. It looked at me and I saw the fury in its eyes. It sprung its hands at me and yelled the word *mittent*. It tried to throw me to the ground by telekinesis, but I moved only a couple of inches.

The surprised shifter yelled the word a few more times at me but was in disbelief when the telekinesis spell to move me didn't work. The shifter then yelled *rigescunt indutae* to freeze me in my place, but I was only slightly frozen. I could still move some parts of my body and wasn't as immobile as before.

It was then that the shapeshifter looked in disbelief at me.

"No. It can't be. How the hell are you immune?"

I gave a mean, wicked smile to the shifter and shrugged. It felt so good to know that Cassandra's negation spell worked. I just didn't know if it would last long.

"Sorry, bitch. It looks like magic is on my side tonight."

The angry shifter shook in rage and clenched its fists. Seconds later, the shifter unclenched its fists and spouted its claws from its fingers. It shined its sharp prickly teeth at me with a strong, penetrating look of madness in its eyes. It was then that I looked down at the iridium sickle I had in my hand and gripped it tight.

I looked at the shifter with squinted eyes before I charged at it.

"Ready for round two?"

The monster and I both charged at each other. But we both stopped in our places when we heard the loud howling of a wolf. The shifter's anger intensified, and it didn't take long for Derek to suddenly appear from a group of trees and ambush the shifter in his wolf form. I could see the slobber coming from his fangs and he was ready to shred the shifter's skin to pieces. Derek tackled the shapeshifter to the ground and pounced on it in a matter of seconds.

I could sense anger and frustration coming from Derek as he sunk his canine fangs into the shapeshifter's jugular veins. I knew the anger was stemming from me ignoring him and destroying the friendship we had together. He took his anger out on the shapeshifter and kept biting into the throat of the shifter, thinking he would kill it. But all the shifter did was writhe in agony. It couldn't scream because Derek might have destroyed its voice box.

The shifter fought back against Derek by slashing

and piercing his fur with its claws and even scratched him on his face. This caused Derek to let go of the shifter's throat and the shapeshifter pushed the were-wolf off of it. After being let go by Derek, the shifter's throat started to slowly heal, which allowed it to whisper the word *mittent* and throw Derek several feet away to the ground.

I looked at the scene happening in front of me, and I was too confused about what to do. I saw the shifter looking at me as the wound in his throat healed gradually and its voice box returned. It wanted to do something to me. But it made the wise move to flee into the depths of the dense forest, thinking that it will hatch a plot to end my life the next time we meet.

I looked at Derek once the shifter was gone from my sight, and I heard him whimper at me. He got up from the ground, where I saw claw marks on his face and blood on his fur. I was a little worried he was severely injured. But then he was able to walk on his four legs and did so towards me. I shook my head and walked away from him, because he was trying to use his whimpering and sad little wolf eyes to soften me up to forgive him. But I wouldn't fall for it.

"Ericka."

I stopped in my tracks when Derek called my name. I turned around and saw that Derek changed back to his human form, wearing only some ripped up jean shorts. He looked at me with intense, passionate eyes like he was determined to do something – to win me back. The scratches on his face and the claw wounds from the shifter self-healed immediately while Derek looked at me like he was in a lot of emotional pain.

"Please talk to me."

"I didn't need your help. I had the shapeshifter right where I wanted it. I can't even look at you right now, Derek. You've hurt me in an awful, despicable way."

"I know. You made that very clear to me. You've been ignoring my text messages. But now that we're both here, face to face, I have the chance to explain everything."

"I don't want to hear it. I'm not in the mood to talk to you right now so just leave me alone. I don't need your help because I can fight my own battles now."

I began to walk away and out of the forest. But Derek had other plans and stopped me from going any further when he ran in front of me. I took a few steps back from him.

"I'm not going anywhere. I'm not giving up on you. On us."

19

"Excuse me?"

"I said, I'm not giving up on us. I'm not going anywhere until you hear me out."

"May I remind you that I have a freakin' sickle in my hand made out of iridium? I'm not afraid to use it on you if I have to! If it weakens shapeshifters, it must weaken werewolves!"

Derek snatched the sickle from my hand in a moment of defiance and gripped the iridium blade in his hand. He didn't feel any pain at all, and my sickle had no effect on him.

"Yeah, iridium doesn't weaken us."

He tossed my sickle back at me and I caught it by its handle. I looked at Derek with a vengeful, hateful pair of eyes.

"What do you have to say after you made me feel humiliated and stupid by lying to me about what you really are? After everything you've done to me, what do you have to say for yourself now, Derek? I can't wait to hear your sad, pathetic excuses!"

"I'm not the monster you think I am!"

"What's the difference between you and the shifter? Other than being two races of monster, you're still a monster just like the one I'm hunting! And you lied about being a werewolf, which is the worst part! I feel like you did all those kind and wonderful things for me, so you can have a pass for what you did!"

"What? What are you talking about? No, that's not it at all, Ericka! I would never, ever do that to you! Ericka, I thought we were friends! Every time you battled the shifter, who would come to your rescue? Who would help you when the shifter had you down and was about to kill you?"

I shook my head and just threw my hands in the air. I started to walk away from Derek in a random direction in the forest. I tried to look for a way out and pondered which direction would take me to my car. All of these thoughts ran in my mind as I felt Derek behind me, pursuing me and trying to clear everything between us.

"Ericka, you're being selfish right now and you're not giving me a chance to make it up to you!"

"Why should I?"

"Because I have a heart and I care about you! Ericka, please! Hear me out!"

I wanted to walk away so bad and never look back. I just wanted to find my car parked outside the forest and leave Derek in the dust. But something inside me pulled me towards him. It was like he had a magnet hidden underneath the six-pack abs on his torso. Something inside me pulled me towards him and made me want to hear what he had to say.

"Ericka, please. Turn around."

I was hesitant to turn around, but I had to so I could hear him out. I didn't need to owe him the opportunity to make things right for me, but I felt like he deserved a chance to defend himself. I turned around and looked at Derek, whose eyes were squinting, and his lips were stretched out to his cheeks. I looked at Derek and crossed my arms, still feeling somewhat bad for not allowing him a chance at redeeming himself. I stared into his eyes with a serious look.

"When I met you at school during lunch, I considered it to be the luckiest day of my life. You were this beautiful, lovely girl sitting all by yourself with nobody to keep you company. I took it upon myself to sit with you and get to know you, and then we developed this warm, growing friendship that I wanted to protect and preserve because it meant so much to me."

I almost wanted to blush from what Derek said. I looked down at the ground for a second before raising my gaze back to Derek.

"If you knew I was a monster, a werewolf, you would never talk to me again. You would never be with me or associate yourself with me again. That's why I lied. Ericka, I love our friendship and what we have had together so far. I didn't reveal my identity as a werewolf to ruin such a lovely friendship that we built that day during lunch at school. My worst fears came true that night you discovered I was a wolf. The day that I feared the most came that night and I was just so heartbroken after you left me like that. I felt so horrible and so much sorrow in my heart."

I unfolded my arms and wiped my face from the small drops of tears that rolled down my cheeks. Derek cried as he said all those words to me, and I couldn't help but feel terrible for treating him the way I did. No werewolf or monster in this world would ever have a heart like Derek and would express their feelings the way he did. In fact, I didn't think all monsters had feelings, until I saw the one standing right in front of me.

"I have a human heart. I'm not the monster you think I am. Just because I'm a werewolf, it doesn't mean I'm devoid of all human emotions. Please try to understand that. I would never hurt you or lay a finger on you. I saved you from the clutches of that wretched shifter every chance I could."

I nodded and kept wiping some tears away from my cheeks with the sleeve of my cotton blue sweater.

"I know. But what hurt me the most is that you lied to me and broke the trust I had in you. You betrayed me in the worst way possible. I felt like you had committed a crime or a sin."

"I know. I understand that. I can't apologize to you enough for what I did. I can't do enough from now forward to try and make it up to you. But Ericka, your forgiveness means so much to me. Please, I promise to never lie or betray your trust in any way ever again. Can you just please forgive me?"

I didn't answer Derek's question instantly. I looked all around me at the landscape and looked up at the night sky hanging above Appleton. I started to rub my eyes over the exhaustion my body felt from the battle with the shifter and all the talking between Derek and me. I placed my left hand inside my pocket while bending the right one holding the sickle behind my back.

"It's getting late, Derek. Can we talk about this later?"

"Sure! Take all the time you need. I understand."

"We can meet up at the park tomorrow. How's that?"

"I love that. Thanks."

I nodded some more and wiped the last remaining tears from my face. I began to walk away from Derek and only turned around to say good night to him. I saw him wave goodbye and say it in a low, pessimistic voice. It was like he didn't think I would forgive him in the end. But he gave me a lot to think about for the remainder of the night. He made me feel so bad about myself, like I couldn't look at a mirror because I would see a cruel person looking back.

I sat on my usual bench at the park the next morning. I was handed the night shift at my job today, so I decided to meet with Derek before I went there. It was a little cold, so I decided to wear my thickest hoodie in the closet, along with my warmest leather winter boots. I tucked my hands in my pockets and looked at the cold coming out from my nose and mouth. I neglected to bring my gloves with me because I was somewhat sleepy. I didn't wear the talisman on my neck, opting instead to hide it in my room where no one would see it. I'd have to make up a story for it later on.

I saw Derek walking towards me with his hands placed in the pockets of his long denim jeans. He wore a large black overcoat with a wool scarf and a red beanie on top of his head. He was a few feet away from the bench when he recognized me by the long blonde hair flowing out from underneath my hoodie. He looked at me with a warm smile on his face.

"Hey, Ericka. How're you doing?"

"Good, how about you?"

"You agreed to talk to me and see me, so I'm feeling happy. I haven't felt that way these past few days."

I gushed on the inside, but I didn't show anything on the outside except for a lukewarm smile. Derek wanted to sit down but was reluctant. It's like he needed my permission to sit because he may have wanted to give me space.

"Can I sit next to you?"

"Please do."

He sat down in an eager way and looked at me with the same bright, warm smile he had when he looked at me. I maintained the same mild smile, being careful not to give him any expectations. I didn't want Derek to think he was getting away with what he did by agreeing to meet him and talk to him.

"So, what's on your mind? Did you think about what I told you last night?"

"I did. First, I wanted to say sorry for not giving you any chance to defend yourself or explain yourself. I'm also sorry for ignoring your messages."

"Water under the bridge as far as I'm concerned. I just want your forgiveness. Whatever I can do to earn it, I will. Just name it."

"Make no mistake about it. I'm still feeling a little grudged because you lied to me about being a werewolf. I'm certainly not going to let you get away with your actions, either. The trust I have in you is near zero right now and you have your work cut out while rebuilding it back up."

Derek nodded and looked at the concrete ground underneath our feet. He had a dismal look on his face that told me I was being harsh on him again. I felt bad in my heart for that, and I tried to rectify the situation at the moment.

"But you've proven to me you're not a monster and that even though you're a wolf, you still have a heart and a human side to you. I know that now. You're also very sincere about your apology and your words when you say you want to earn back my forgiveness and make it up to me."

It was then that Derek looked up from the ground at me with his bright green eyes widened. A smile started to curve on his lips as they parted.

"Are you saying –"

"What I'm saying is that we can still be friends. You are partially forgiven for now. Like ten percent. But I'll be able to forgive you more with time."

The full smile I expected showed on Derek's face and I could feel he was happy for the first time in days. I saw a little twinkle in his eyes like he wanted to cry again. He tried to hold back his emotions and tried to talk while avoiding a quaver in his words.

"Thank you so much. This means so much to me. You have no idea how much I appreciate you, Ericka."

"You're welcome."

It was then that the lukewarm smile I had on my mouth was now bigger in size. I looked at Derek with my own bright smile and I could tell it made his day even better.

"So now that we're starting fresh, there's an idea I have for making it up to you."

"What's that?"

"Movie night tomorrow, at my cabin."

I shook my head while still retaining the smile on my face.

"I don't know. Your cabin?"

"We could go to a theater if you want! It'll be my

treat and you get to pick the movie you want to watch. How's that?"

"I have to balance my job with the mission to hunt down and kill the shifter."

"Well, now that you and I are good again, you're no longer alone in your mission. I'm more than happy to help you kill that monster once and for all. All in good time. But for now, please let me take you to a movie. Please?"

I couldn't help but succumb to Derek's begging. I relented and we agreed to a movie tomorrow night. I was able to do it since I was part of the day shift crew the next day.

"I need to tell you something, though."

"What's that?"

"So, I kind of told my friends a big lie about you."

Derek sat up on the bench with a look of concern on his face.

"What did you say?"

"No, Derek, it's okay. I promise I'll fix it. I'll make it right, okay?"

"I believe you. What did you say?"

My cheeks grew red with embarrassment. I felt horrible for lying about Derek to my friends and I was almost reluctant to tell Derek.

"I may have told my friends that you were a sore loser after our bowling game, you accused me of cheating and we got into a big argument, you yelled and cursed at me and I did the same to you, and..."

I left Derek in suspense as he looked at me with shock and anger in his eyes.

"Well, come on! Spill it!"

"I told my friends that you disrespected my dead parents by saying they would be proud of how they raised a cheater."

Derek's eyes and mouth widened to the fullest extent. I avoided Derek's gaze and displayed my own look of nervousness while he gawked at me with a shocked and angered expression.

"Ericka! Why would you say that? I would never be a sore loser and I would never curse at you! I certainly would never disrespect your parents! That's awful, why did you lie about me like that?"

"It was my own payback for your lies to me! Look, I'm sorry, okay? I'll make things right and I'll make something else up to MacKayla and the others."

"So, you're going to lie even more?"

"You don't get to judge me based on lies."

With an annoyed look on my face, the anger and awe on Derek's started to fade. He saw I had a point.

"Okay, fine. I just want things to be right between us. I hope they are."

"They will be."

Derek nodded and smiled at me, which made me return it somewhat to him.

"I can't wait to see you tomorrow," he said.

"Me, too."

Derek came closer to me and gave me a hug. I wrapped my arms around his massive back and rubbed it a few times. The hug lasted for a couple of minutes and I wasn't ready to let him go just yet. I was absorbing all the warmth and comfort from Derek and it felt good to just melt my stress and bad vibes in his arms. Besides, the more I held Derek in my arms, the more I was willing to forgive him and consider the decision to move on.

20

Today was dominated by Derek making it up to me for his lies. We went to a movie theater to see a movie of my choosing, which was a romantic comedy. I haven't been in the theater for so long. When I walked into the theater, a feeling of nostalgia overcame me when I smelled the stale odor of reconditioned air combined with buttered popcorn, hotdogs, nachos, and Coke.

Derek bought a large popcorn for both of us and two medium-sized fountain drinks. When I insisted on buying a pair of hotdogs with my own money, he took the cash from my hands and playfully placed them back in the pockets of my camo green leggings. He paid for my two hot dogs and we went to the theater.

Derek and I wound up eating the majority of our food before the movie began. I munched down my two hot dogs before the second to last trailer could even come on screen. Our two drinks and the tub of popcorn between the two of us was almost gone by the first half of the movie.

When the movie ended, Derek came up with the idea to go somewhere and get a bite to eat. We both felt hungry after finishing our snacks early in the movie. He decided to take me to Steak Shack, a fast-food chain I had never heard of before.

"They sell the best Steakburgers anywhere in the U.S.," he said.

My face warped into a look of pure cringe and disgust. I felt like I gained twenty pounds just by hearing that word. An image of cow beef and steak combined ran through my mind and I pictured fatty grease dripping down its side.

Steakburger?

"I don't think I want to go to that place. It sounds like two animals got murdered just to make that burger."

"Oh, come on. You've never heard of a Steakburger?"

"No, and there's a good reason why, too."

"Lighten up, will you? It's not like that. Come on, let me take you there and I promise you it'll be the best burger you've ever had.

"To you it will be. But I don't think so for me."

I could tell how bad Derek wanted to make it up to me by treating me to his Steakburgers at Steak Shack. I couldn't say no so when I relented, he almost jumped up with joy. It was like a win-win situation for him. He would have his favorite meal while thinking he would be getting in my good graces.

We entered a Steak Shack restaurant and saw the place was almost filled up. These 'steakburgers' must be very popular for people to fill up a place like this so I thought maybe they weren't that bad. Derek didn't even look at the menu before him and I went up to the counter and he ordered what he wanted.

"I'll have a Triple Steakburger with cheese fries instead of the original fries, and I'll also have a red velvet milkshake."

I looked at Derek with my eyes near the edge of their sockets and a wide gaping mouth. I looked at the menu just to see if he was messing with me. I saw a thumbnail of the sandwich Derek ordered and the image I had in my mind before multiplied by three. If one patty inside two buns was bad, three was ghastly.

Triple Steakburger?

I thought that maybe because Derek was a wolf, he may have wanted to satisfy his animal cravings. It made all the sense in the world to me once I considered that I was standing next to a colossal werewolf.

"What are you looking at me like that for? This is just like McDonald's, except there's steak involved!"

I shook my head and looked at the menu. Then I looked into the eyes of the girl that took our orders. She wore her ink black hair in a ponytail while wearing a Steak Shack cap. I looked into her dark brown eyes and gave her my order: chicken fingers with fries and an Orange Fanta.

"Wait a minute, stop."

Derek gave me a look of confusion mixed with annoyance. His eyes were squinted while his lips were slightly open, as if he questioned why I wanted this order.

"I brought you here to try a *Steakburger*, not some chicken fingers. Come on, Ericka. Loosen up a little."

"I don't think I'll like it, though. I've gotten used to normal patties at any other fast-food chain. But steaks and burgers don't go together."

"Please. Come on."

Derek took me to the side while he grabbed my hands. He leaned closer to my ears and began to speak.

"I'm trying so bad to make it up to you for my stupid actions. I want to know that my efforts aren't in vain because I really care about making things right with you, Ericka. I want our friendship to thrive. Please, try to have a good time and loosen up a little. It's my treat so you don't have anything to worry about. Just try it for me. Please?"

He backed away and I nodded while looking at the ground for a small second. I looked back at Derek and saw a warm smile on his face. It was contagious and I looked back at him in the same way.

"I know, I really appreciate it. I know you're sincere about it…okay, I guess I'll try a Steakburger. For you. You are such a sweet guy, so I'll do it for you."

The smile on Derek's face grew and it felt a little good to make him that happy. Derek reinforced my gut feeling that he meant well and that he was adamant about making our friendship work. We both went back to the counter and saw a couple of people waiting behind us, looking at Derek and I with annoyed expressions. I felt slightly embarrassed and hurried to the counter, where I ordered a Bacon Cheese Steakburger with fries and a Kit Kat milkshake.

"That's it! It wasn't so hard, now was it?"

I shook my head, and we went to a side area to wait on our meals.

"So, how are you able to pay for our movie, snacks, and our meals here? I feel bad if you're spending money on me and you don't have a job."

"No, I do work. I'm a mechanic at an auto parts shop. I balance that with school and running errands for the house. And I also balance it with…you know, my nighttime activities under the moon, especially a full one."

Derek looked away from my gaze and down to the floor. He rubbed his spiky hair and twitched his legs. I know what he's referring to. He just didn't want to say it because he focused on making these right with me and may have felt that rehashing the issue wouldn't be a great idea.

"Oh…yeah, I know. So, I didn't know you were a mechanic. Do you like doing that?"

"Oh, it's a great job for me. I like to study all vehicles and their parts. It's like studying the human anatomy, but instead of studying bones, muscles, and every part of the body, I look at the 'skeleton' of a car or a motorcycle. It's like being a doctor for vehicles. It's really good."

"I'm glad you like it. It's awesome that you're working."

There was a brief moment of silence between Derek and I before he had anything to say.

"What about you? Are you looking for a job or have you found one already?"

"Yes, I work at this place called Riley, Jr.'s. It's pretty chill and I'm getting the hang of it."

"That's good. I think I heard of that place."

"It's a food chain but not major or anything. It's more community-oriented."

Derek nodded and looked at the floor with a light smile on his face. I avoided his eyes and looked around at the lively place. Our order was then ready, and we took the food to Derek's truck. We ate it all in there and even made a mess of Derek's seats. But he reassured me that he'd make some time later to clean everything up.

"All that matters is that you had a good time today."

"Thanks. I did. I hope you did, too."

There were a few moments of silence between us before I saw a troubled look on Derek's face. He looked down at his fingers as he intertwined them with one another.

"Derek? Is there something wrong?"

Derek looked up and gave me a smirk while he tightened his lips.

"Yeah, it's just…I realized something."

"What is it?"

"We have one more thing in common."

"What's that?"

"You remember what I told you a while back when you were staying at my cabin recovering from your injuries? I told you that I knew what it felt like to lose someone violently."

My mind raced to that day and I remembered it well. I was in one of Derek's bedrooms in the cabin and he told me that he experienced the same type of loss I experienced. I remember him leaving the room without telling me anything about what he meant. Now, after all this time, I would get to know the answer to that mystery.

"Yeah, I remember."

"Well, I was talking about my parents. They died violent deaths."

I gave Derek a look of surprise.

"Are you serious?"

"Yeah. My dad was shot during a hunting trip, and my mom took her own life soon after."

My eyes expanded to the maximum and I covered my wide-open mouth with my hands. Derek grew a look of sorrow on his face and looked down at his fingers again.

"Oh my gosh! That's awful, Derek, I'm so sorry!"

I leaned over to Derek and comforted him by giving him a hug that was as tight as I could make it. My legs were placed awkwardly on the passenger seat as I leaned over to Derek and grabbed his upper back and shoulders. Derek held me in the middle of my back while turning his body at an angle.

I felt so much sympathy for him. All this time I was mad at him and being so harsh on him. I couldn't help but cry at that moment because I felt so guilty for treating Derek like that before I felt so much compassion for what he went through. Derek let go of me and started to wipe my tears away.

"Hey, hey! Why are you crying?"

"I just feel so awful for the way I've treated you before. You and I have faced tragedy in our lives, and we've got so much in common. But I've been pushing you away and I'm really sorry for that."

"No, Ericka, don't be sorry, alright? You pushed me away because you were mad at me for lying to you. You thought that I betrayed you and you were hurt so I understand. Please stop crying, alright?"

But I couldn't help it. I just continued crying when I felt Derek lean against me and wrap me tight in his arms. I felt the warmth of his body as it soothed me, and my tears stopped rolling down my cheeks. I couldn't feel anything but admiration and appreciation for Derek for being so kind and forgiving towards me. The fact that we both had members of our family die cruel, unexpected deaths pulled us closer together.

Our hug ended and I smiled at Derek while he wiped a few more tears from my face.

"Do you forgive me?"

"Of course! There's nothing to forgive."

"So…do you know who killed your dad? Did they catch the killer?"

Derek didn't answer me. He bent his head down and rubbed his neck before sighing and looking up at me. He grabbed my hand and flashed a small grin.

"I rather not talk about it anymore. I'll tell you someday."

I nodded and took my phone out of my pocket. I saw the time was almost ten as I wiped all my tears away. Derek took me home, which was something I wanted to avoid. He insisted on picking me up at the end of my shift after Mrs. Devereaux dropped me off in the morning. My car experienced engine problems and she told me her husband, Todd, would take the car to a shop. Derek picked me up from work and I changed my clothes in the bathroom at the restaurant.

I told him my concern about being seen with him in front of Devereaux's house when I haven't fixed my lie and told the people around me, I was friends with Derek again. I came up with the idea of Derek dropping me off a block away from the house, but he wanted to drop me right in front of the house for my safety.

"It's not safe for you to walk through your neighborhood at this time of night."

"Nothing's going to happen."

"You don't know that for sure. Please, I'll drive away as fast as possible. I wanted to give you a hug before I drop you off, but I guess it won't happen."

Derek made a flustered look on his face and looked down at the steering wheel. I couldn't help but feel warm and fuzzy inside.

"I'm sorry."

"No, no. It's silly. I'll drop you off in front of your house and leave immediately. I won't just let you walk through the neighborhood at night. Too risky."

I sighed and smiled at Derek. I didn't have the energy to argue with him, so it was easy for me to give into his demand. Derek executed the plan and drove off into the distance the instant I got out of his truck. I walked up to the front door as if nothing had happened.

The next morning, I slept peacefully in bed while the sun was out. But I woke up to the sound of knocking on my door, which made me grunt and struggle to open my eyes.

"Ericka? You awake?"

MacKayla's voice gave me enough energy to wake up and get out of bed to answer the door. I saw a serious look on MacKayla's eyes, like something bad happened.

"Hey," I said sluggishly. "Everything alright?"

"No. We need to talk."

MacKayla walked into my room without any invitation. She sat on the side of my bed and motioned for me to sit by her. I walked up to my bed and sat beside her. I looked at my best friend and she maintained that grave look of worry on her face.

"Is something wrong?"

"Yes. It's you."

"Me?"

"Yeah. I saw you with Derek last night."

My eyes enlarged. Even though I just woke up and didn't get to wash my face, I was able to widen them after being surprised by what MacKayla said.

"What are you talking about?"

"I saw you and Derek in his truck. Please don't tell me that you're friends with this guy again."

"How do you know it was Derek and not a guy from my work?"

"I looked outside the window and I saw him. I have good eyes and I also…I may or may not have some binoculars in my room."

A look of irritation appeared on my face.

"You were watching me?"

"I was worried about you. You didn't get home until past ten. Don't turn this around on me. Were you with Derek last night or not?"

I took my eyes off of MacKayla and looked down at the floor. I picked my nails a little, afraid to answer her question. But my silence pretty much answered MacKayla's question and I picked my head up to see that she looked at me with a look of shock on her face. She placed her hands on her mouth in disbelief.

"Oh my gosh…you're friends with that guy again? After what he did and said to you? You're back with this guy?"

"Look, he made it up to me, okay? He made it up to me in his own way, sort of."

How did Derek make it up to me? Think, girl.

"What did this guy say or do to make you forgive him for disrespecting your parents and swearing at you?"

"He…he said that his parents, who are also dead, are rolling in their graves over how their son turned out. It was like him making up for disrespecting me about my parents. He was sweet over how much he said sorry, and he took me out to a movie and Steakburgers at this place called Steak Shack, which I had never heard of."

"So that's it? He gets away with disrespecting your deceased parents and yelling and cursing at you like an animal?"

"He's not an animal and I just said that he said his dead parents wouldn't be proud of him for the way he turned out. It was like making it up to me for what he said. Come on, MacKayla. Everyone deserves a second chance. I'm a forgiving girl. My parents taught me to be that way."

MacKayla looked away from me and shook her head. She had a look of anger on her face while she stared at my bedroom door. I looked down at my lap and picked up my nails some more. I looked at her and she turned to face me.

"I was so confident you would leave this guy. You even said you would never see him again and you told him you weren't friends again."

"I know but things change in life. He even got me this."

I thought about my talisman that I bought from Cassandra's shop. In case MacKayla ever saw it and asked me about it, I had a good story for her. I took it out from a drawer in the nightstand beside my bed. I showed MacKayla the pendant and she looked at it with a cringed expression.

"He got you this?"

"Mhm."

"That's the ugliest necklace I've ever seen in my life. If he was going to make it up to you, at least he should have had the decency to get you something more beautiful and valuable. And why does it have so many creepy markings on it? It looks like it belongs in a witch's house or something."

"It doesn't matter! Ugh, it's a talisman and it's something he thought was cool for me to wear. Besides, it's not about the worth of the gift. It's about the gesture. He's not a millionaire. He's a mechanic."

MacKayla rolled her eyes and shook her head.

"Can you give him another chance? Please? For me."

MacKayla looked at me with a modest smile. She took my hands and held them.

"Okay. For you, honey. But if he does anything

stupid again, you let me know so I can find him and butcher him. Deal?"

I laughed a little and nodded at my best friend and sister figure.

"Deal."

21

The library wasn't all that busy today. There were a lot of tables that were empty and none of the computers had their screens on. I sat at a table near the back of the library, in a secluded area where no employee was working or doing anything in that area. I carefully chose this spot because I was meeting up with Derek today.

I needed absolute privacy if him and I were going to discuss our next plan of action against the shapeshifter. We would have chosen the park or anywhere more private and secluded than the library. But it was too cold to go to the park and the warmth of the library was the perfect solution for that. No other place would have been that much more private than the library because it had less people than a coffee shop or a café.

I proposed to Derek that we simply meet up in his cabin, but he dismissed the idea because he came up with the excuse that his cabin was too filthy and didn't want me to think he was a slob on purpose. Derek told me that he was doing a bunch of challenging home-work and needed comfort food to get through it. He told me he ate so much that he wound up making a big mess of the living room and didn't want me to see it.

How much comfort food did a werewolf need? Obviously, plenty.

We had no choice but to come to the library and it was difficult to find a spot for us to talk without any interruptions and talk in a low voice where no one would hear us. I had to choose the next best thing, which was a desk in a corner near an old bookcase in the reference books section of the library.

I sat by myself, smelling the dust and wood of the books and shelves near me. I also couldn't help but smell some of the lavender air freshener plugged some-where in the library. It was fighting with the smell of the books and hardwood bookcases for dominance of the library's air and atmosphere.

I waited almost fifteen minutes from the time I came to the library. I then saw Derek walk over to my desk after probably spending some time looking for me in the library.

"It's about time you showed up."

"Sorry, Ericka. I had to clean up the living room a little bit and I had to deal with some traffic. I also looked for you in the library. You really chose this spot carefully."

Yeah, I figured.

Derek leaned in and held my shoulders in his arms

while I was seated, and he was standing. I held Derek on his sides and felt how hard and firm his muscles were. It was right near his abs and I figured that his abs must have been ten times stronger and meatier than the rest of his body was. Laying my fingers on Derek's hips near his ab area made me sweat and my heartbeat faster than usual.

"It feels so good that I can finally do that again," Derek said.

"I know. I missed it too, to be honest, when we weren't talking."

Derek let me go and looked at me with a look of surprise.

"You mean that?"

"Yeah. I mean I have to say, given your size, you give one of the warmest hugs I ever feel."

Derek flashed a big smile on his chiseled face, and I smiled back at him, feeling good over how I made him feel good.

"I'm glad to hear that," he said.

"Alright so we have a lot to discuss with this shifter."

The smile from Derek's face faded quickly and it was replaced with a sterner look. I wanted to switch the topic to talk about the shifter and it was like he was hit out of the blue with my shift from talking about his hug to all of a sudden starting to talk about the shifter. He nodded and looked at me with a more serious face, thinking that he could no longer enjoy my compliment to him about how fine his hugs are.

"Right, of course. Back to business."

I leaned closer to Derek so we could talk in a low voice. I didn't want any word from our conversation to suddenly be heard by anybody in the library. I didn't care how alone we were in the corner. I couldn't take any risk from our conversation being leaked outside Derek and I's private bubble. He leaned in closer to meet my gaze and hear me well.

"We need to find a way to kill this thing. I'm tired of it fleeing from us and surviving every time we face it. Its heart is obviously not in its chest like I thought it would be. The weapons we have simply weaken it, but we need to *kill* it."

"I wish I had a solution, but we need Bart's book. There's simply no way we can defeat the shifter without Bart Ramsey's book, and it could be anywhere in the country."

"That's the least of our problems right now. This shifter knows some dark magic, too. It's bad enough that we have to deal with its raw strengths. But we can't deal with the dark magic spells the monster has in its knowledge."

Derek took his eyes off me and leaned away further from me. He sat back in his chair and looked at the desk, his brain thinking about the last confrontation with the shapeshifter. I could tell he thought about the Latin phrase that the shifter yelled at him to throw him off of it. He looked back at me after growing a look of concern on his face.

"You're right. I heard the shifter say this weird word. I couldn't understand it, but it was from a foreign language. It screamed the word at me and the next thing I knew, I was tossed into the air several feet away from it."

"I know. It's because it was a telekinesis magic spell that the shifter knows. And that foreign language is Latin."

"Wait a minute. How do you know they're magic spells?"

Derek then looked down at my chest and saw the talisman. I wore it today to show it to him but I was careful to tuck it inside my shirt so no one else would see it.

"Where did you get that?"

"Okay, I should tell you everything. When you and I weren't talking to each other, I found a magic shop where I found out a former witch worked. She enlightened me on witches and told me things that blew my mind away."

"What? There's a witch in Appleton?"

"Yes. Well, former witch. She wanted to be, but she got kicked out of an academy."

"What did she tell you?"

"She told me how there were white witches and black witches, how black witches are evil and white witches are good, and other things that just mesmerized me."

"Oh, yeah. I could've told you about that if you would've talked to me. I know about white and black witches."

"But then I told her about my situation and she gave

me two things. One is a negation spell that allowed me to block all the dark spells that the shifter threw at me. The other is this talisman that allows humans to cast witch spells, so they don't suffer any side effects from magic. Monsters don't need it because they can handle the side effects. I got the talisman from her and the sickle you saw me hold in my hands that night."

Derek nodded and looked at the floor of the library for a brief minute before he looked into my eyes again.

"That's great. I'm glad you found a helpful resource to help you when you were alone, and I wasn't there to help you."

Derek looked at the people in the library and at the books near us to avoid looking at me. I sensed that he felt awful for what he did to me that caused me to shun him from my life, which led me to being alone and having to deal with the shifter on my own.

"Derek, it's okay. It's in the past. Whatever problems you and I had, they're in the past. Let's just focus on the present and dealing with this shifter."

Derek looked back at me and nodded.

"Okay. We need a plan to end this shifter's miserable life. I get that. But without Bart's book, we're left to weaken it instead."

"I had a plan to just stab the shifter all over its body until I struck its heart."

"But that's haphazard, though, and not really a good plan when we're dealing with a shifter. Besides, it knows magic so I'm glad you found that witch...well, former witch, and got a negation spell from her. You could've been seriously hurt trying to execute that plan on your own."

"I know, but I have you now. We need to work together. How about you and I use the negation spell to block the dark magic spells from the shifter? Then, we can wound it all over its body until we find the heart and destroy it."

It was then that Derek entered a deep mode of thought. He was searching all the corners and crannies of his werewolf brain for any solutions he could tell me about it. His eyes then widened, and he made a sharp turn of his head towards me.

"I have an idea that isn't as risky as yours, but it can be effective."

"What is it?"

"How about if we sever the claws of the shifter? Think about it. The claws are the shifter's main weapon. It can't kill us if we de-claw it. If we cut off the shifter's claws and we both use the negation spell to block all of the shifter's dark spells, it'll definitely give us more time to find Bart's book!"

I thought about Derek's idea for a few minutes. I turned my gaze towards the ground as my brain worked to wrap itself around Derek's idea to absorb and understand it. I looked at Derek with a question on my mind.

"How long will it take for the shifter to grow back new claws? If it can self-heal, surely it has the power to generate a new set of claws."

"I don't know, but it can be a while. I know it causes

shifters so much pain when they don't have claws. All I know is that it will buy us a lot of time to find the witch who was Bart's friend and she'll lead us to the book."

"But how are we going to do that?"

"We can just go back to the former witch you found at the magic shop and consult her about it. In the meantime, we need to de-claw that shapeshifter and weaken it to the point it'll be fully incapacitated for a long time. Then we find Bart's witch, get the book, and end that shifter's life. What do you say?"

I nodded in approval at Derek's plan. I smiled at him and told him verbally that I approved. He smiled at me and it felt so good to know that we were on the same page.

22

The Magic Witches' Bazaar was five minutes away. I drove Derek and myself to the shop so he could meet Cassandra. The car ride was spent mostly talking about our jobs and his school as well as the shapeshifter. We also listened to a few tunes on the radio. Derek kept changing stations every time a song came on that I liked but he didn't. It was annoying at first until I saw him smiling at me and I knew he was just being playful.

"So, what should I expect from meeting this former witch?"

"Well, she's pretty chill for someone who used to be into magic. I think she still is, but obviously not like deep, deep into it, you know? She got kicked out of a witch academy for being too weak to handle true magic."

"I can't believe there are academies for witches. As a

werewolf, I'm not aware of that much information about them. Only the basics."

"Care to enlighten me?"

"No, it's not important. We just need to focus on the shifter and killing it. I'm sure this witch will help us. How did you even find her?"

I looked at Derek as I balanced the gaze of my eyes towards him and the road. We were like two minutes away from the shop and there wasn't much traffic to deal with.

"One, her name is Cassandra. Two, I found her on Google."

"Google? Supernatural creatures aren't that existent on the human internet, let alone witches."

"I searched up the term 'magic shop' and there she was, the first result on the first page."

Derek chuckled and shook his head. He looked out the window to see if we were there yet, like a child on a vacation to Disney. The shop was on my right when we arrived. Derek studied the building as I parked the car in a random spot. The lot was empty, and it was like no one came to the store. They didn't take it seriously and they only looked at it as an antique show, not an actual shop for magic and the supernatural.

Derek and I got out of the car and went inside the shop. Derek looked at everything around us, from the same creepy dolls, idols, statues, and skulls I saw my first time here to the herbs, incense, plants, and oils stored in jars and containers on plenty of shelves.

Derek picked up his nose and smelled the air of the shop to get a feeling for it.

I could tell Derek didn't have a favorable impression of the place. Even as a werewolf, he found the shop to be too ghastly for his taste.

"Geez, where did this lady get all this stuff? I feel like I'm in a scene in a commercial for Halloween Horror Nights."

"You're a werewolf and you find this shop to be creepy?"

"Just because I'm a wolf, it doesn't mean we find everything in the supernatural world to be mundane. Like I told you, I have a human side to me."

"Uh-huh. Yeah, okay."

Derek smiled and snickered at me while nudging me in my elbow. We both walked up to the counter and I pressed the button to get Cassandra's attention. I wondered where she was and what she was doing. Maybe she worked on creating some spells from the books she stole from that academy. She could also be cleaning and organizing a secret stash of items in the back. Whatever it was, it sure kept her occupied in the back or maybe some secret room in the shop.

Derek and I heard footsteps coming from behind the wooden bead curtain that led to another section of the shop. I could see Cassandra's silhouette in the dark hallway through the curtain. More of her features appeared as she got closer to the curtain. Cassandra went through her curtain and had a smile on her face with a look of surprise.

"Ericka."

"Hey, Cassandra."

"This is a lovely surprise. What do I owe for this spectacular visit?"

"Cassandra, I like you to meet my friend Derek."

Derek had a light smile on his face and waved at Cassandra. A jubilant look Cassandra had a few seconds before when she greeted me slowly faded away as she looked at Derek.

"Hi," Derek said.

"Cassandra, Derek's –"

"A werewolf. Let me guess, the werewolf who saved you from the shapeshifter?"

I looked at Derek with a stunned expression on my face. He looked at me in the same way and I also saw some confusion mixed in his bright green eyes. I looked back at Cassandra and saw her looking at me with squinted eyes and a meager grin.

"Yes. How do you know?" I asked.

"Just because I'm not a witch, dear, it doesn't mean I can't sense a monster or know a spell or two."

Derek bobbed his head and rolled his eyes. I saw the look on his face shift to one of irritation, like he wanted to punch Cassandra in the face. He turned towards Cassandra with his eyebrows inched closer together and his lips gaping.

"Okay, you know what? We don't need to use the M word, okay? Yes, I'm a werewolf. But I'm not that much of a monster. So, just don't use the M word."

Cassandra nodded and she had an unimpressed look on her face.

"Uh-huh. Right. So, you're just a cuddly, soft werewolf, aren't you?"

Derek started fuming and he turned his attention towards me.

"Alright, I can't do this, I don't like her already. Let's just go and find a witch or former witch that's more hospitable and not rude."

I gave Derek a mean look to try to calm him down. Cassandra watched this interaction and she suddenly grabbed Derek's hands. A confused Derek looked at her and wondered what she was doing, and so did I.

"Derek, I'm just kidding. I'm messing with you. It's very nice to meet you. I sensed you were a werewolf, and I used the opportunity to take a crack at you. But I'm sorry, I realized we got off on the wrong foot here. Do you accept my apology?"

Derek didn't answer Cassandra's question immediately. He turned towards me with a stern look plastered on his face while Cassandra still held his hands in an awkward way. He turned his gaze back to Cassandra and looked at his hands in hers. The size of Cassandra's small, tiny hands holding Derek's bear paws was just a cute sight in my mind. It was like a Chihuahua trying to calm a Great Dane.

"Alright. I accept your apology."

The atmosphere in the shop turned into a positive, warm one. Cassandra let go of Derek's hands and gave him a warm, motherly smile. He couldn't help but smile a little back at her after Cassandra's grin was infectious. I even beamed at the sight of those two becoming friendly.

"Wonderful. Now, Ericka. Tell me why you're here."

"Derek and I are here for some more weapons and we need you to make two of those negation spells for the both of us."

"Certainly. I forgot to ask. What happened in your battle against the shapeshifter after the last time I saw you?"

"Well, I used the negation spell you gave me along with the talisman, and they worked like a charm. I was able to have more power over the dark spells that the shifter tried to use against me. And I had no side effects when I recited the negation spell thanks to the talisman. Now I need two of the same spell for Derek and me. He's in on the fight with me against the shapeshifter. We're also here for some weapons."

"Very well. What type of weapons do you need?"

"Mainly silver and iridium," Derek interjected.

"Yeah, my machete became useless when the shapeshifter used some type of spell and melted the silver. I didn't think it was possible. Silver doesn't melt that easily, which means it must've been some pretty strong heat."

"Yes, I suppose so. Anyways, I'll be right back."

Cassandra walked through the wooden rod curtain and came back out with a long wooden box that had some weird seal carved on top of it. Cassandra opened the box and revealed two medium-sized silver spears sitting atop a red folded cloth. It was a hypnotic sight as Derek and I studied each detail of the weapons.

The shafts of the spears were made of hard wood and there were three of the same sigils on the box carved on the handles of both spears. The blades were double-edged and sharpened carefully to the tips. Cassandra returned through the curtain to the back of the store and stayed there for about fifteen minutes. Derek and I were amazed by the beauty of the spears and kept staring at them the entire time Cassandra was gone.

She returned with two slips of paper containing the negation spells for Derek and me to use. We bid farewell to Cassandra and left her shop with our newest weapons. Outside, while Derek and I got in my car after placing the negation spells inside the box with the spears and putting it in the back of my car, he gasped, and I looked at him with an expression of concern on my face.

"What's wrong?"

"Nothing! I just got an idea of what else we can do to really weaken the shifter!"

"What's that?"

"What if we tried severing its spine? I don't how much pain it'll cause it exactly or what kind of impact it will have on the shifter, but it's worth a try and I want to do it, obviously because I'm the wolf."

I thought about Derek's idea for a minute as I looked at my steering wheel. I looked back at Derek and met his eyes.

"Yes, I think it's certainly something worth trying."

23

I t was battle time for Derek and me. We both said the negation spells Cassandra gave us in our vehicles parked outside the forest's edge. Derek and I met there, and we walked almost a mile into the forest, keeping our eyes sharp and focused for any signs of the shapeshifter. I wondered in my mind why Derek didn't shift. He was usually in his wolf form by now, but he was still human.

Maybe he wanted to wait for the shapeshifter to show up and then transform. But I got the feeling that he didn't shift because I was there, and he didn't want me to see him become a wolf. But I didn't concentrate on it too much. I had one dominant thought in my mind and that was the shifter. I held one of the silver spears Cassandra gave us along with the iridium sickle while Derek held the other spear.

Derek and I walked through the forest looking for it, but all we could see were the vast numbers of trees in front of us and heard nothing but the hooting of owls and other birds. We also heard the crunching of leaves and the forest's earth beneath our feet, something that we wanted to reduce to not make our presence known that much. Wherever that bastard shifter was, we wanted to catch it off its guard.

I looked at Derek on occasion and he looked more laser focused than I was. I could tell he was trying to zero in on the shifter's location using his supernatural wolf senses, even though he wasn't in wolf form. This was my mission and my battle against the shifter, but his efforts to help me out made me think he was more after the shifter than me. He was so dedicated to helping me find and kill this thing that I thought the shifter killed a relative of his too. I appreciated all of his efforts and one day, I might just show him my gratitude.

"Are you picking up on anything yet?"

Derek shushed me with his briefly parted lips and a motion from his left index finger. He then began to look around him with widened eyes and a pricked-up nose.

"The more talking we do, the less I can find this shifter with my senses."

"Wouldn't it be easier if you transformed into a wolf?"

Derek didn't offer an immediate answer. I saw a slight red hue on his chiseled cheeks when I asked him that question. It was then that I knew in my mind for sure Derek was scared to transform in front of me. His forehead reflected a little bit of light from the moon, where I could see some sweat forming near the edge of his hair.

The weather wasn't that hot or humid. Instead, the sweat on Derek's forehead formed from some nervous feelings he had.

"Are you scared to turn into a wolf in front of me?"

Derek bowed his head to the ground and swiveled his head towards me for only a second. He was subconscious about turning into a wolf in front of me and it only confirmed it even more in my mind. He didn't want me to see him become the monster I knew he was, and I just felt so bad at the moment over how much I called him a monster and rejected him because of it.

"Let's just find the shapeshifter. The less we talk, the better and sooner we find and kill it."

"Alright."

I looked down at the ground as Derek and I walked deeper into the forest. I had an upset look on my face and a gut-wrenching feeling inside. I felt like a horrible, pathetic person for judging Derek so much about his identity as a werewolf and I was willing to bet that the first interaction between him and Cassandra played constantly throughout his mind. He probably tied those thoughts with me and didn't want to turn into a wolf because of that.

The shame of being such a bad person consumed my mind as Derek continued our trek through the forest. I picked my head up and took my eyes off the ground, and looked at Derek. I saw him more flustered than before. I could tell the topic of him transforming in front of me threw him off. He was less concentrated and more nervous, which was an added insult to the guilt I already had in my mind.

But everything changed with one sudden sound. All the guilt and shame I felt inside was now gone. All the thoughts and feelings I had now faded. Derek and I had vigilant, surprised looks on our faces when we heard a tree near us shaking and one of its branches snapping from the heavy weight of something on it. Derek and I heard a thud on the ground after that.

Whoever broke the tree branch with its weight must have climbed that tree in the first place and was now on the ground. The thud we heard sounded like a pair of feet landing on the forest earth and Derek looked around for the source of the sound with his green eyes wide apart and his lips parted just as wide. He used his wolf senses more than ever and sensed that something was close.

"Get ready," he said.

I gripped my weapons in both my hands tight and I saw the spear in Derek's right hand wrapped firmly in it. We both looked around us and stood stationary in our place. Soon enough, we heard footsteps walking through leaves and I could see a silhouette walking towards us from some trees in the distance.

"Well, well, well…if it isn't the odd couple."

The shapeshifter flashed its prickly teeth in a disgusting taunting smile towards us. The monster was initially in Derek's appearance. It took one look at me and its skin changed, its eyes changed, every feature of it changed to my appearance. It looked at Derek with its sadistic eyes, ready to spew more barbs from its lips.

"Aww, what's wrong, puppy? Can't seem to shift in front of your girlfriend? Are you scared of her?"

"Shut the hell up, or you'll regret it."

"Wow, big words coming from an incompetent, impotent little mutt. You've always managed to save your princess but couldn't find a way to quite kill me."

The shifter took its gaze off of Derek and turned its attention to me. It looked at me with a pathetic but very wicked grin. I looked at it with a stern expression of anger and vengeance, wanting to rip its heart out wherever it was in its grotesque, deformed true shape.

"And you…you can't fight your own battles, so you hire this dog to help you? You're the one who wants revenge for the death of your aunt. I see no involvement for him."

"That's where you're wrong. Maybe if I was a monster like you, I would take you out on my own. Maybe I will rip you to shreds and send you to wherever pathetic afterlife you belong in. But lucky for you, I'm just human. But even while I'm human, I still have magic, a pair of weapons, and a werewolf on my side. So, your pathetic life on this earth is up. At least it'll be that way very soon. And I will have justice for my aunt and every human you killed."

The shifter no longer looked at me or Derek with a stupid smile plastered on its face. A more annoying, somber look took over its imposter face. I could see the shifter shaking a little with its fists clenched by its sides. It drew its claws out from its fingers within seconds. It must've been provoked from the reminder of the last time it tried to use its dark magic on me and failed miserably.

"Enough talking," the shapeshifter remarked.

It stretched its hands out while looking at Derek and I with hatred and rage flaming in its eyes. The shifter started to bend its fingers in a grip-style gesture, similar to a Darth Vader choke.

"*Suffoco*," the shifter yelled.

Derek and I started to feel our insides tighten a little and tingle. It was like the shifter trying to choke us or our insides. But the negation spells proved effective once again and we barely felt any effect from the shifter's latest spell. At that point, the shifter put its hands down and maintained that same level of anger at its magic being thwarted from Cassandra's negation spell once again.

"Negation spell. Once again. So, the two of you are now protected by it, huh? And you have that stupid necklace to protect you from magic, too."

Derek and I couldn't help but flash smiles at each other before looking back at the shifter.

"One, it's a talisman, and two, you don't have a problem with that, do you?" I asked with a sarcastic tone.

"Yeah, I mean if this is how the whole night is going to go, I'm going to be bored," Derek interjected.

"And I rather have some fun by ending your miserable life."

The shifter kept the same stern look on its face as we taunted it. It felt good to throw some insults at it for once and it was equally good to see its reaction. But the mood all changed when the shifter started smiling at us. It then began to laugh as Derek and I looked at each other, confused and wondering what the hell was going on. The shifter stopped laughing and turned to us, the happiness and smiling on its face shifting gradually to a more serious look.

"You want fun, Derek? I'll give you fun. And no, it's not a problem, Ericka. Because I have a *solution*. You see, you two clowns think you have me all figured out…well, I'm going to prove you so, so pathetically wrong."

The shifter stretched its hands out once again. All of its fingers and claws pointed straight towards Derek and me as the shifter peeled its lips back once more.

"*Maximum magica potentia absoluta in tenebris, ego perdere a vestra virus negationis inutilem reddere.*"

Derek and I began to feel tingly sensations coarse through our bodies. It was like we were weakened by something, another spell that the shifter just said. Our muscles, veins, and nerves began to feel like some weight was lifted off of them. At that point, the shifter smiled one more time and stretched its hands out, with both its fingers and claws pointing straight at us.

It started to walk closer to us and the closer it inched to us, the more nervous we got. It was about fifteen feet away from us. Now it was more like eight. The shifter grew enough confidence to be near us considering we had weapons ready in hand to strike against it. Whatever Latin phrase it said earlier gave it some boost of power.

"*Suffoco!*"

The shifter bent its fingers in the same grip gesture from earlier and started to squeeze them. Both Derek and I started to painfully gasp for air as we felt our internal organs being choked and crushed with every corresponding movement from the shapeshifter's fingers. The Latin phrase it said earlier must have destroyed the negation spells Cassandra gave us, an obvious explanation that ran in my mind as I felt my life being pulled out of my body.

The shifter then smiled and clenched its fists while it held it hands out in the air. The pain and damage it caused to our insides made Derek and I fall to our knees as we both felt helpless against this new power of the shifter. All I thought was who was going to save us and that if we did survive this ordeal, we would find the black witch who supplied the shapeshifter with these dark spells and crush her with our bare hands.

The shifter bent to the ground in the middle of Derek and me as we writhed in pain and tried to somehow release ourselves from the magical grip inflicted on us.

"Now I get to end both of you and put you out of your misery for good."

I couldn't tell if the shifter was looking at me

because my eyes were teary and closed from trying to handle all the pain.

"Say hi to your aunt when you see her."

I managed to turn my head around and opened my eyes slightly to see Derek was being suffocated as painfully as I was. But then, I saw him stare at the moon. He was staring at it so intensely; it was like he was trying to use it as some power up for his werewolf abilities. I started to see a shift in Derek's body.

Even though he was in a lot of pain like I was, Derek's body began to change shape. The more his eyes fixated on the moon, the more he was able to change his body. I heard bones snapping out of place and I saw Derek lose more of his human appearance. His jaws got larger, and his sharp fangs emerged out of his teeth. His black shirt, leather jacket, and jeans began to shred, too.

Derek's skin soon changed to black fur, his head and skull changed to that of a wolf, his body shrunk to the size of a wolf, and his hind legs emerged out of his human legs. Finally, the tail sprouted from his rear end and Derek changed into his wolf form. The shapeshifter released its grip and looked at Derek with horror in its eyes. I crawled away from both of them as I tried to catch my breath and absorb all the oxygen I could from the forest.

I crawled to a nearby tree, and I looked at what occurred in front of me. Derek panted heavily and wagged his tail in every direction while flashing its fangs at the shifter and directing a look of deep anger and unlimited fury at the shifter. The shifter looked horrified at the werewolf and shook its head in disbelief.

"No, no...no! It's not possible!"

Derek stopped panting once his breathing readjusted to its normal pace. His tail stopped moving and he just looked at the shapeshifter with boiled blood and volcanic rage. Within a matter of seconds, Derek pounced on the shifter and began clawing at its face with his claws. Derek even jabbed the shifter in both of its eyes with his claws.

There was no stopping Derek once he was blanketed with wrath and all that was on his mind was tearing the shifter into a million pieces. After scratching and clawing the shapeshifter to a bloody pulp, Derek rolled the shifter on its stomach using its claws and nose. Derek sunk his teeth and clawed into the back of the shifter in a frenzy, at which point I knew what he was doing.

"What if we tried severing its spine? I don't how much pain it'll cause it exactly or what kind of impact it will have on the shifter, but it's worth a try and I want to do it, obviously because I'm the wolf."

"Yes, I think it's certainly something worth trying."

I remembered those words in my mind as I saw Derek rip apart the skin on the shifter's back to try and sever its spinal cord. I was breathing normally by that point and was back to a hundred percent. While the shifter was writhing on the ground screaming, I took the opportunity that presented itself right in front of me.

I pounced right off the ground and ran to one of the silver spears I saw in the distance. I grabbed one of the grounds and ran to the shapeshifter, where I started severing each of its claws with the spear. Its loud screams pierced both my ears, but I kept my focus targeted on the claws of the shifter and I cut off all ten of its claws.

Derek had managed to sink its teeth and claws into the spinal cord of the shifter by the time I was done. But the shifter didn't die. Soon after Derek was done with his work, the shifter crawled at an inhuman rapid pace from both Derek and I on its legs and hands. It fled deep into the dense forest where Derek and I no longer saw it.

I sat on the ground next to Derek and saw blood all over his mouth and the fur underneath it. He crawled to me and began to whimper like a little dog at me. He placed his head on my lap and looked at me with his bright green canine eyes. I couldn't help but be over-whelmed by how cute he was when he sat on me in his wolf form. I started to pet his fur and the more I petted it, the more I began to be comfortable with Derek's identity as a werewolf and the more I got to accept him for who he was. I was also extremely happy that we managed to declaw the shifter and get a major victory.

"You did a good job, Derek. You saved both of us. I can't thank you enough for transforming. You did it, buddy. I'm so proud of you."

Seconds later, I no longer felt Derek's fur on my lap, or his canine head. They disappeared from in front of me. Instead, I looked to my side and saw Derek back to human form sitting right next to me, naked and his butt touching the soggy dirt of the forest.

"We did it, Ericka. As in you and me. I don't deserve all the credit you know."

"Yeah, but you shifted to a wolf just in time to save us from the magic spell of the shifter. We could've been dead by now. You have saved both of our lives."

I saw Derek's dimpled cheeks begin to blush and he had a bright smile on his face.

"Thanks. But you declawed the shifter and accomplished what we set out to do."

I nodded and looked at the ground with a smile on my face. I looked back at Derek and couldn't help but blush when I looked into his bright green eyes and chiseled six-pack abs that adorned his torso. But then I thought about the negation spell and the smile and blush I had on my face were gone. I gave Derek a confused look.

"How was the shapeshifter able to block our negation spell? I thought it was supposed to be effective. Now it's useless to us."

Derek adorned the same puzzled look I had.

"I don't know, to be honest. My guess is that there are no magic spells that are more powerful than others."

"What do you mean?"

"Like, there are no magic spells that have unlimited

power. It seems like in the world of magic, every spell has an answer to it and there are spells in the magic world that block other spells. You know what I mean?"

I nodded to answer Derek's question. I looked down at the ground as I tried to make the best of his explanation, but it only made me even more confused about magic.

24

I parked my car outside of Angelwood High School and looked at the exterior of all the adjoining buildings. I haven't been here in so long and looking at the school brought so many memories back to my mind. I sat in my car waiting for the dismissal bell to ring and thought about all the days during lunch time where MacKayla, Hillary, and I sat together and had the greatest times ever.

All the topics we talked about, from our classes, assignments, other girls, boys, movies and TV shows, celebrities, and everything in between came back to my mind. I knew there was nothing that would bring those times back to me. But I had solace knowing there was a place preserved in my mind for them. From freshman to junior year, those times of bliss will always live in my memory lane as well as my heart.

The dismissal bell rang, and I was looking for Derek

to come out of those doors any minute now. I came to Angelwood to surprise him and I parked my car near his truck so that it would be hard for him to miss me when he came to his truck. A wave of students hurried out of the doors of the school.

I got out of the car and looked for Derek in between the students who were walking out. I recognized Maisy as she walked out of the doors while she talked to a pair of her friends. I knew I would see her and interact with her another day. After a few minutes, I was able to see Derek walking out of the door after recognizing his height and spiky hair. Derek walked over to his truck near my car. He looked in its direction and surprised when I waved at him.

Derek saw me and had a huge smile on his face. He ran over to me and when he came up to me, he held me in his arms, and I felt the warmth of his body toward mine. His body was like a source of sun rays radiating off of him as I wrapped my arms around his shoulders and felt his smooth hair on mine. I had to reach up on my tippy toes to meet the level of his head.

"Oh my gosh, this is such a nice surprise!"

"How are you, Derek?"

"Ugh, I'm doing so much better now that I saw you!"

"I'm glad."

The embrace between us ended but Derek still held my hips in his oversized hands while I still had mine on his biceps. Derek studied me and what I wore, which was a red floral summer dress underneath a denim jacket and a pair of canvas slip-on sneakers.

"You are just too beautiful for words."

"Aww, thanks. You're so sweet."

"To what do I owe this surprise visit?"

"Well, I just thought I would come by and take you to a special place. I need to talk to you about something."

Derek made a fascinating look on his face, widening his eyes as he looked into mine and stretching his lips to the sides. He let go of my hips and I let go of his vast muscles.

"A special place, huh?"

"Yes. I need you to follow me with your truck. I really want to get there, okay?"

Derek nodded in response to what I said, maintaining that smile on his face.

"Sounds good. I'll be right behind you."

"Awesome!"

Derek and I got in our vehicles and I drove to a lake near the forest. He followed close behind my car on the road and even parked right next to it when we arrived at the lake. We both got out of our vehicles and I saw a confused look on Derek's face.

"This is the special place you brought me to?"

"Yes."

"I don't see what's so special about a lake."

"Well, it's not the location that's special but rather what's going to happen by the lake that will be special."

A look of intrigue came across Derek's face as I grabbed him by his hand and dragged him to the edge of the lake, where we both sat down.

"So, what do you want to talk about? And what's this special thing that's going to happen?"

"All in good times, Derek. First, I need to talk about us and the status of our friendship."

I looked into Derek's eyes and I saw he began to worry about what I was going to say. I immediately placed my hands on top of his and sought to remedy his worries.

"Don't worry. It's good. I'm going to talk about something wonderful regarding our friendship."

Derek nodded and said, "Okay."

"So, you know how I've been friend-zoning you ever since I met you because I've told you that I wasn't ready for a relationship?"

"Yes, I remember that very well. And I told you that I understood because I'm an understanding guy. You told me about the death of your mother and then your aunt got murdered so I still understand if you're not ready for a relationship."

"Yeah, but see, here's the thing…"

I couldn't immediately say it to Derek. I was flustered as I looked at the lake in front of us, not knowing how to break the news to Derek. I avoided his gaze as much as I could while I thought of the best way to speak my mind to Derek and say what I had to say.

"Ericka? Is everything alright?"

"Yeah, I'm just struggling to tell you something."

"It's alright. You can tell me anything in any way."

Derek scooted closer to me and wrapped his right

arm around mine while he rubbed my left forearm with his left hand. I felt more comfortable from the touch of his fingers enough to start saying what's on my mind in the best way possible.

"Lately I've just seen how sweet you are and how much you've proven to me that despite being a were-wolf, you just have such a good heart. I've also felt safer around you and warm and comfortable. Throughout our friendship, you've saved me countless times from the shapeshifter, including two days ago when you transformed in the nick of time to save both our lives."

I looked at Derek and saw a big beaming smile on his face. This encouraged me to keep going.

"Even though you kept the fact you were a werewolf from me in the most deceptive way possible, you more than made it up to me, especially when you helped me get vengeance for my aunt against the shifter. I feel like ever since we made up, our friendship has grown."

Derek continued to rub my left forearm but with more speed this time. It was like my words encouraged him to give me more comfort.

"I'm glad, Ericka. And I'm truly sorry for lying to you about being a werewolf and making up a child-hood friend."

"It's alright, you don't have to be sorry anymore. Ever since we met, I've been putting you in the friend zone. But now I feel like our friendship has grown. I've been rethinking the status of our friendship and I believe it's time to take it to the next level, if you agree."

A shocked look invaded Derek's face. I saw the pupils of his bright green eyes dilate and his lips peel back to a gaping hole. He stopped rubbing my arm and let go of me.

"The next level? You mean –"

"A relationship. A couple. Boyfriend and girlfriend. You and me. What do you say?"

Derek's shocked look morphed into one of utter joy. He almost wanted to cry over what I told him and looked at the lake in disbelief. He turned back to me with his widened green eyes.

"So, this was the special thing you were planning?"

I nodded to answer Derek's question. He continued to look at me in disbelief.

"I've been keeping you at arms' length for so long that I think it's time to take our friendship to another level. Let's experiment and see where our relationship takes us. What do you say?"

"I say, Ericka Jones, I would be more than happy to be your boyfriend."

Derek leaned in close to me and placed his lips on mine. His right arm tucked on my hair while he placed his left arm centered on my back. I held him in the same way, and we kissed each other like we had nothing else to do for the rest of the afternoon. The uninterrupted sounds of nature and the water of the lake rippling in front of us filled our ears. Just like these sounds were continuous, so was the passionate kiss I shared with my new boyfriend.

Follow Ericka and Derek's story in SHIFTER DAMNED and book two of the Appleton Wolves Trilogy! Get it on Amazon!

Printed in Great Britain
by Amazon